THE
DROVER'S
WIVES

Published in 2019
by Lightning Books Ltd
Imprint of EyeStorm Media
312 Uxbridge Road
Rickmansworth
Hertfordshire
WD3 8YL

www.lightning-books.com
ISBN: 9781785630910
Copyright © Ryan O'Neill 2019

First published in Australia by Brio Books, 2018

Cover by Ifan Bates

British Library Cataloguing in Publication Data
A catalogue record for this book is available from the British Library.

Printed by CPI Group (UK) Ltd, Croydon CR0 4YY

101 REINTERPRETATIONS OF

THE DROVER'S WIVES

HENRY LAWSON'S AUSTRALIAN CLASSIC

RYAN O'NEILL

*To Henry Lawson
and Raymond Queneau*

The Drover's Wife xi

1. Table of Contents 1
2. Hemingwayesque 3
3. Tanka. 7
4. A Year 8 English Essay 8
5. List of Ingredients. 11
6. A Cryptic Crossword 12
7. A Child's Drawing 17
8. An Agony Aunt Column 18
9. Sporting Commentary 20
10. A Disease. 26
11. Lipogram. 28
12. Freudian 30
13. A Mixtape 31
14. A 1950s Children's Book. 32
15. McCarthyesque 35
16. Parable. 38
17. Editorial Comments 39
18. A Children's Toy 42
19. Elizabethan 43
20. Lecture Slides 48
21. A Gossip Column 54
22. Glaswegian 56
23. A Self-Published Novel Cover 58
24. Cento. 59
25. A Pop Song 62
26. A Fine Wine 65
27. A 1980s Computer Game .66
28. Yoked Sentences 70
29. A Dance. 73
30. A School Play 75
31. Cosmo Quiz 79
32. Political Cartoon 83
33. A Fable 84

34. Emojis 85
35. Backwards 87
36. A Card Game 89
37. Horoscope 91
38. Clichés 92
39. Tweets 95
40. A Question Asked by an Audience
    Member at a Writers' Festival 99
41. Verbless 102
42. An Amazon Book Review .104
43. A Choose Your Own Adventure Book 106
44. Limerick 114
45. An Abstract Painting 115
46. Penthouse letter 116
47. An Insurance Claim 120
48. A Real Estate Advertisement 122
49. Songs from a Broadway Musical 123
50. Pangram 125
51. A Comic Strip 126
52. Sensory 128
53. Interrogative 132
54. Stream of Consciousness .135
55. Onomatopoeia 137
56. Chronological 139
57. A Reality TV Show 142
58. Epic 149
59. Maths Problems 152
60. An RSPCA Report 155
61. A Letter to the *Daily Telegraph* 157
62. A Movie Review 158
63. Wordcloud 163
64. Sex Manual 164
65. Hangman 168
66. Monosyllabic 169
67. Meme 171
68. A Golden Age Detective Novel 172
69. Imagist 179
70. Ocker 180
71. A Self-Help Book 183

72. A Spam Email 185
73. Punctuation 188
74. Conditional 189
75. An Absurdist Play 191
76. N + 7. 195
77. Endorsements. 196
78. Scratch and Sniff 199
79. TV Guide. 200
80. Spoonerisms. 203
81. Contemporary 205
82. Lovecraftian. 207
83. Abecedarian 210
84. Imperative. 212
85. Internet Comments 214
86. Fill in the Blanks 218
87. Finnegans Wife 220
88. Classifieds. 222
89. Bar Graph. 226
90. Trivia Questions. 227
91. Academese 229
92. Bush Ballad 233
93. Biographical. 236
94. Univocalic. 242
95. Wordsearch 244
96. A Crass American Sitcom 245
97. Postmodern 255
98. Bibliography. 258
99. Index. 260
100. A Note on the Type 263
101. Paint Swatches . . . . back cover

The Drover's Wife

by Henry Lawson

The two-roomed house is built of round timber, slabs, and stringy-bark, and floored with split slabs. A big bark kitchen standing at one end is larger than the house itself, veranda included.

Bush all round — bush with no horizon, for the country is flat. No ranges in the distance. The bush consists of stunted, rotten native apple-trees. No undergrowth. Nothing to relieve the eye save the darker green of a few she-oaks which are sighing above the narrow, almost waterless creek. Nineteen miles to the nearest sign of civilization — a shanty on the main road.

The drover, an ex-squatter, is away with sheep. His wife and children are left here alone.

Four ragged, dried-up-looking children are playing about the house. Suddenly one of them yells: 'Snake! Mother, here's a snake!'

The gaunt, sun-browned bushwoman dashes from the kitchen, snatches her baby from the ground, holds it on her left hip, and reaches for a stick.

'Where is it?'

'Here! gone into the wood-heap!' yells the eldest boy

— a sharp-faced urchin of eleven. 'Stop there, mother! I'll have him. Stand back! I'll have the beggar!'

'Tommy, come here, or you'll be bit. Come here at once when I tell you, you little wretch!'

The youngster comes reluctantly, carrying a stick bigger than himself. Then he yells, triumphantly:

'There it goes — under the house!' and darts away with club uplifted. At the same time the big, black, yellow-eyed dog-of-all-breeds, who has shown the wildest interest in the proceedings, breaks his chain and rushes after that snake. He is a moment late, however, and his nose reaches the crack in the slabs just as the end of its tail disappears. Almost at the same moment the boy's club comes down and skins the aforesaid nose. Alligator takes small notice of this, and proceeds to undermine the building; but he is subdued after a struggle and chained up. They cannot afford to lose him.

The drover's wife makes the children stand together near the dog-house while she watches for the snake. She gets two small dishes of milk and sets them down near the wall to tempt it to come out; but an hour goes by and it does not show itself.

It is near sunset, and a thunderstorm is coming. The children must be brought inside. She will not take them into the house, for she knows the snake is there, and may at any moment come up through a crack in the rough slab floor; so she carries several armfuls of firewood into the kitchen, and then takes the children there. The kitchen has no floor — or, rather, an earthen one — called a 'ground floor' in this part of the bush. There is a large, roughly-made table in the centre of the place. She brings the children in, and makes them get on this table. They are two boys and two girls — mere babies. She gives them some supper, and then, before it gets dark, she goes into the house, and snatches up some pillows and bedclothes — expecting to see or lay her hand on the snake any minute. She makes a bed on the kitchen table for the children, and sits down beside it to watch all night.

She has an eye on the corner, and a green sapling club laid in readiness on the dresser by her side; also her sewing basket and a copy of the Young Ladies' Journal. She has brought the dog into the room.

Tommy turns in, under protest, but says he'll lie awake all night and smash that blinded snake.

His mother asks him how many times she has told him not to swear.

He has his club with him under the bedclothes, and Jacky protests:

'Mummy! Tommy's skinnin' me alive wif his club. Make him take it out.'

Tommy: 'Shet up, you little ——! D'yer want to be bit with the snake?'

Jacky shuts up.

'If yer bit,' says Tommy, after a pause, 'you'll swell up, an' smell, an' turn red an' green an' blue all over till yer bust. Won't he, mother?'

'Now then, don't frighten the child. Go to sleep,' she says.

The two younger children go to sleep, and now and then Jacky complains of being 'skeezed.' More room is made for him. Presently Tommy says: 'Mother! listen to them (adjective) little possums. I'd like to screw their blanky necks.'

And Jacky protests drowsily.

'But they don't hurt us, the little blanks!'

Mother: 'There, I told you you'd teach Jacky to swear.' But the remark makes her smile. Jacky goes to sleep.

Presently Tommy asks: 'Mother! Do you think they'll ever extricate the (adjective) kangaroo?'

'Lord! How am I to know, child? Go to sleep.'

'Will you wake me if the snake comes out?'

'Yes. Go to sleep.'

Near midnight. The children are all asleep and she sits there still, sewing and reading by turns. From time to time she glances round the floor and wall-plate, and, whenever she hears a noise, she reaches for the stick. The thunderstorm comes on, and the wind, rushing through the cracks in the slab wall, threatens to blow out her candle. She places it on a sheltered part of the dresser and fixes up a newspaper to protect it. At every flash of lightning, the cracks between the slabs gleam like polished silver. The thunder rolls, and the rain comes down in torrents.

Alligator lies at full length on the floor, with his eyes turned towards the partition. She knows by this that the snake is there. There are large cracks in that wall opening under the floor of the dwelling-house.

She is not a coward, but recent events have shaken her nerves. A little son of her brother-in-law was lately bitten by a snake, and died. Besides, she has not heard from her husband for six months, and is anxious about him.

He was a drover, and started squatting here when they were married. The drought of 18 — ruined him. He had to sacrifice the remnant of his flock and go droving again. He intends to move his family into the nearest town when he comes back, and, in the meantime, his brother, who keeps a shanty on the main road, comes over about once a month with provisions. The wife has still a couple of cows, one horse, and a few sheep. The brother-in-law kills one of the latter occasionally, gives her what she needs of it, and takes the rest in return for other provisions. She is used to being left alone. She once lived like this for eighteen months. As a girl she built the usual castles in the air; but all her girlish hopes and aspirations have long been dead. She finds all the excitement and recreation she needs in the *Young Ladies' Journal*, and Heaven help her! takes a pleasure in the fashion-plates.

Her husband is an Australian, and so is she. He is careless, but a good enough husband. If he had the means he would take her to the city and keep her there like a princess. They are used to being apart, or at least she is. 'No use fretting,' she says. He may forget sometimes that he is married; but if he has a good cheque when he comes back he will give most of it to her. When he had money he took her to the city several times — hired a railway sleeping compartment, and put up at the best hotels. He also bought her a buggy, but they had to sacrifice that along with the rest.

The last two children were born in the bush — one while her husband was bringing a drunken doctor, by force, to attend to her. She was alone on this occasion, and very weak. She had been ill with a fever. She prayed to God to send her assistance. God sent Black Mary — the 'whitest' gin in all the land. Or, at least, God sent King Jimmy first, and he sent Black Mary.

He put his black face round the door post, took in the situation at a glance, and said cheerfully: 'All right, missus — I bring my old woman, she down alonga creek.'

One of the children died while she was here alone. She rode nineteen miles for assistance, carrying the dead child.

It must be near one or two o'clock. The fire is burning low. Alligator lies with his head resting on his paws, and watches the wall. He is not a very beautiful dog, and the light shows numerous old wounds where the hair will not grow. He is afraid of nothing on the face of the earth or under it. He will tackle a bullock as readily as he will tackle a flea. He hates all other dogs — except kangaroo-dogs — and has a marked dislike to friends or relations of the family. They seldom call, however. He sometimes makes friends with strangers. He hates snakes and has killed many, but he will be bitten some day and die; most snake-dogs end that way.

Now and then the bushwoman lays down her work and watches, and listens, and thinks. She thinks of things in her own life, for there is little else to think about.

The rain will make the grass grow, and this reminds her how she fought a bush-fire once while her husband was away. The grass was long, and very dry, and the fire threatened to burn her out. She put on an old pair of her husband's trousers and beat out the flames with a green bough, till great drops of sooty perspiration stood out on her forehead and ran in streaks down her blackened arms. The sight of his mother in trousers greatly amused Tommy, who worked like a little hero by her side, but the terrified baby howled lustily for his 'mummy.' The fire would have mastered her but for four excited bushmen who arrived in the nick of time. It was a mixed-up affair all round; when she went to take up the baby he screamed and struggled convulsively, thinking it was a 'blackman;' and Alligator, trusting more to the child's sense than his own instinct, charged furiously, and (being old and slightly deaf) did not in his excitement at first recognize his mistress's voice, but continued to hang on to the moleskins until choked off by Tommy with a saddle-strap. The dog's sorrow for his blunder, and his anxiety to let it be known that it was all a mistake, was as evident as his ragged tail and a twelve-inch grin could make it. It was a glorious time for the boys; a day to look back to, and talk about, and laugh over for many years.

She thinks how she fought a flood during her husband's absence. She stood for hours in the drenching downpour, and dug an overflow gutter to save the dam across the creek. But she could not save it. There are things that a bushwoman can not do. Next morning the dam was broken, and her heart was nearly broken too, for she thought how her husband would feel when he came home and saw the result of years of labour swept away. She cried then.

She also fought the pleuro-pneumonia — dosed and bled the few remaining cattle, and wept again when her two best cows died.

Again, she fought a mad bullock that besieged the

house for a day. She made bullets and fired at him through cracks in the slabs with an old shot-gun. He was dead in the morning. She skinned him and got seventeen-and-sixpence for the hide.

She also fights the crows and eagles that have designs on her chickens. Her plan of campaign is very original. The children cry 'Crows, mother!' and she rushes out and aims a broomstick at the birds as though it were a gun, and says 'Bung!' The crows leave in a hurry; they are cunning, but a woman's cunning is greater.

Occasionally a bushman in the horrors, or a villainous-looking sundowner, comes and nearly scares the life out of her. She generally tells the suspicious-looking stranger that her husband and two sons are at work below the dam, or over at the yard, for he always cunningly inquires for the boss.

Only last week a gallows-faced swagman — having satisfied himself that there were no men on the place — threw his swag down on the veranda, and demanded tucker. She gave him something to eat; then he expressed his intention of staying for the night. It was sundown then. She got a batten from the sofa, loosened the dog, and confronted the stranger, holding the batten in one hand and the dog's collar with the other. 'Now you go!' she said. He looked at her and at the dog, said 'All right, mum,' in a cringing tone, and left. She was a determined-looking woman, and Alligator's yellow eyes glared unpleasantly — besides, the dog's chawing-up apparatus greatly resembled that of the reptile he was named after.

She has few pleasures to think of as she sits here

alone by the fire, on guard against a snake. All days are much the same to her; but on Sunday afternoon she dresses herself, tidies the children, smartens up baby, and goes for a lonely walk along the bush-track, pushing an old perambulator in front of her. She does this every Sunday. She takes as much care to make herself and the children look smart as she would if she were going to do the block in the city. There is nothing to see, however, and not a soul to meet. You might walk for twenty miles along this track without being able to fix a point in your mind, unless you are a bushman. This is because of the everlasting, maddening sameness of the stunted trees — that monotony which makes a man long to break away and travel as far as trains can go, and sail as far as ship can sail — and farther.

But this bushwoman is used to the loneliness of it. As a girl-wife she hated it, but now she would feel strange away from it.

She is glad when her husband returns, but she does not gush or make a fuss about it. She gets him something good to eat, and tidies up the children.

She seems contented with her lot. She loves her children, but has no time to show it. She seems harsh to them. Her surroundings are not favourable to the development of the 'womanly' or sentimental side of nature.

It must be near morning now; but the clock is in the dwellinghouse. Her candle is nearly done; she forgot that she was out of candles. Some more wood must be got to keep the fire up, and so she shuts the dog inside and hurries round to the woodheap. The rain has cleared off. She seizes a stick, pulls it out, and — crash! the whole pile collapses.

Yesterday she bargained with a stray blackfellow to bring her some wood, and while he was at work she went in search of a missing cow. She was absent an hour or so, and the native black made good use of his time. On her return she was so astonished to see a good heap of wood by the chimney, that she gave him an extra fig of tobacco, and praised him for not being lazy. He thanked her, and left with head erect and chest well out. He was the last of his tribe and a King; but he had built that wood-heap hollow.

She is hurt now, and tears spring to her eyes as she sits down again by the table. She takes up a handkerchief to wipe the tears away, but pokes her eyes with her bare fingers instead. The handkerchief is full of holes, and she finds that she has put her thumb through one, and her forefinger through another.

This makes her laugh, to the surprise of the dog. She has a keen, very keen, sense of the ridiculous; and some time or other she will amuse bushmen with the story.

She had been amused before like that. One day she sat down 'to have a good cry,' as she said — and the old cat rubbed against her dress and 'cried too.' Then she had to laugh.

It must be near daylight now. The room is very close and hot because of the fire. Alligator still watches the wall from time to time. Suddenly he becomes greatly interested; he draws himself a few inches nearer the partition, and a thrill runs through his body. The hair on the back of his neck begins to bristle, and the battle-light is in his yellow eyes. She knows what this means, and lays her hand on the stick. The lower end of one of the partition slabs has a large crack on both sides. An evil pair of small, bright bead-like eyes glisten at one of these holes. The snake — a black one — comes slowly out, about a foot, and moves its head up and down. The dog lies still, and the woman sits as one fascinated. The snake comes out a foot farther. She lifts her stick, and the reptile, as though suddenly aware of danger, sticks his head in through the crack on the other side of the slab, and hurries to get his tail round after him. Alligator springs, and his jaws come together with a snap. He misses, for his nose is large, and the snake's body close down in the angle formed by the slabs and the floor. He snaps again as the tail comes round. He has the snake now, and tugs it out eighteen inches. Thud, thud comes the woman's club on the ground. Alligator pulls again. Thud, thud. Alligator gives another pull and he has the snake out — a black brute, five feet long. The head rises to dart about, but the dog has the enemy close to the neck. He is a big, heavy dog, but quick as a terrier. He shakes the snake as though he felt the original curse in common with mankind. The eldest boy wakes up, seizes his stick, and tries to get out of bed, but his mother forces him back with a grip of iron. Thud, thud — the snake's back is broken in several places. Thud, thud — its head is crushed, and Alligator's nose skinned again.

She lifts the mangled reptile on the point of her

stick, carries it to the fire, and throws it in; then piles on the wood and watches the snake burn. The boy and dog watch too. She lays her hand on the dog's head, and all the fierce, angry light dies out of his yellow eyes. The younger children are quieted, and presently go to sleep. The dirty-legged boy stands for a moment in his shirt, watching the fire. Presently he looks up at her, sees the tears in her eyes, and, throwing his arms round her neck exclaims:

'Mother, I won't never go drovin'; blarst me if I do!' And she hugs him to her worn-out breast and kisses him; and they sit thus together while the sickly daylight breaks over the bush.

THE
DROVER'S
WIVES

Table of Contents

Chapter I: In which the scene is set, namely an out-of-the-way shack in the Australian bush in the dying years of the nineteenth century

Chapter II: Wherein some child's play is most rudely interrupted by a malevolent interloper

Chapter III: In which both our villain, the black snake, and our heroine, the drover's wife, are introduced, and the manner of their first meeting

Chapter IV: Of the indignities suffered by Alligator the dog in pursuit of his bête noire

Chapter V: In which thunder is heard and lightning is seen and a thunderous decision is not lightly made

Chapter VI: Of the meal the family enjoyed, and its aftermath

Chapter VII: In which the manifold demerits of (adjective) little possums are discussed

Chapter VIII: In which are contained several memories and opinions on the absent drover, by his wife

Chapter IX: Of how the drover's wife passed her nighttime vigil

Chapter X: Which treats of our heroine's melancholy reminiscences, including and not limited to, her early married life, Black Mary, King Jimmy, bushfires, floods and mad bullocks

Chapter XI: Wherein our heroine discovers she has been cheated, and of how weeping can turn into laughter

Chapter XII: In which an old adversary reappears, and battle is joined once more

Chapter XIII: Of the vanquishing of the snake, and its fiery aftermath

Chapter XIV: Wherein the ties of family are reaffirmed

Chapter XV: In which the day begins anew

Hemingwayesque

He was a young boy who lived in a shack in the bush
and he had gone eighty-four days now without taking
a snake. The five of them lived in the shack: the boy,
his mother, his younger brother and his two little sisters. It was very hot and the children played in the dust
while the woman washed up inside. There was bush all
around with hills like red kangaroos in the distance.
On most days the boy looked out there for a snake and
on other days he looked out there for something else.
But he didn't like to think about that.

'Say, Tommy,' his brother said.

The boy took a swig from the tin cup of water and
wiped his lips with the back of his hand.

'Yeah?'

'I saw somethin' move over there. Across the creek
and into the trees.'

'Sure you did.'

'But I—'

'Scram!'

'Alright, Tommy. Alright. I didn't mean nothin'.'

His brother grinned nervously. The boy waited a
moment, shrugged, and went round the corner of the
house. A snake was basking in the sun. It was black

and long and it looked up at him with dead eyes. The boy swore, and took two slow steps backward. There was a stick on the ground they had been using to play 'Soldier's Home' and he squatted down for it.

'Snake, Ma! Here's a snake!'

It was his brother shouting. A moment later the woman appeared, highball in hand. She might have been pretty once, but that was a long time ago.

'Well, well. What have we here?' she said.

'Oh, cut it out,' he said. 'You know what it is. Let me kill it.'

'Alligator!' the woman called. 'Oh, Alligator!'

'He'd let me kill it,' the boy said, and he spat.

The woman looked amused. 'He's not around,' she said.

The dog came from his kennel. It was black with yellow eyes and old. The boy loved it and now he was afraid for it and ashamed of his fear. The dog growled and snapped at the snake and the snake disappeared under the house.

'Well, isn't this too wonderful?' the woman said.

'Would you do something for me now?' the boy asked.

'I'd do anything.'

'Would you please please please please please please stop talking?'

—

It was dinner-time and they were all sitting around the kitchen table pretending that nothing had happened. The kitchen was a clean, well-lighted place and through the window they could see the clouds gathering.

'I'm going to lie awake all night so I can smash that goddamn snake,' the boy said.

'How many times have I told you not to curse?' the woman said.

She put the children to bed.

The boy had his club with him under the bedclothes.

'Ma, Tommy's skinning me alive with his club. Make him take it out.'

'Shut up, you little louse! Do you want to be bit by the snake?'

His brother shut up.

'If you get bit,' said the boy, 'you'll swell up, and smell, and turn red and green and blue all over till you bust.'

'Now then, don't frighten the child,' the woman said and she went and fixed herself a whiskey.

'Will you wake me if the snake comes out?' the boy said. He wondered if he had succeeded in keeping the pleading from his voice.

'Yes. Go to sleep,' the woman said.

She blew out the candle. After a while his brother said, 'I can't stand to think about her waiting in the room and knowing she's going to get it. It's too damned awful.'

'Well,' the boy said, 'you'd better not think about it.'

—

He was awake. The dog was barking and the boy leapt up, grabbing his club. His mother struck at the snake. The boy ran to help her, but she held him back. The boy knew then what guts meant: grace under pressure.

She lifted the snake on the point of her stick and threw it in the fire and watched it burn. The boy and the dog watched too. After a moment he looked up at her and saw the tears in her eyes.

'Mother, I'll never go droving. To hell with me if I do.'

The dog raised his ears.

'Yes,' she said. 'Isn't it pretty to think so?'

And she embraced him and kissed him as the sickly sun also rose.

Tanka

A snake approaches.
The woman and children run
And hide in the house.
Through the long night she watches –
Shedding memories like scales
And the snake burns with the dawn.

A Year 8 English Essay

What narrative techniques does Lawson use to shape the reader's perception of the drover's wife?

'The Drover's Wife' by Henry Lawson (2005) is an Australian novel set in Australia featuring the wife of a drover. It is a historical story. Most historical stories take place in the past, and so does this one. A drover, according to the Oxford English Dictionary is 'one who drives sheep' and a wife is 'a married woman' so as we can see, the themes of sheep and marriage run deep throughout the story. Henry Lawson uses lots of multiple narrative techniques throughout the novel which shape the reader's perception of the drover's wife. For example, flashbacks, description, humour and sadness.

The first technique Lawson uses to shape the drover's wife is flashbacks. The story is set a long time ago with the wife looking back on her life and when a black snake viscously attacked her children. On page three of the story she thinks back to floods and bush-fires and being attached by Aboriginal people. She also thinks about her husband who always treats her like a 'princess.' (Lawson, p.3, 2005). As we can see from this quote, the writer shows us lots of things about the drover's wife's past so we will know more about her past.

Secondly, there is description like 'He is not a very beautiful dog, and the light shows numerous old wounds where the hair will not grow.' (p.5) Here they are talking about their dog Alligator, who has bravely fought the snake and got bit and so his hair is falling out. The quotation, 'Her husband is an Australian and so is she' is also vital, as it lets the reader know that the story is set in Australia, and not America, for example. Finally, an 'evil pair of small, bright bead-like eyes' demonstrates that the snake is evil. Thus, description is an important narrative technique in the book.

Humour is furthermore a vital part of the novel. The drover's wife's children have Asperger's and are comic relief. They say things like 'I'd like to screw their blanky necks' and 'Blarst!' which makes the wife laugh and the reader. Also, the dog is called Alligator, which is a funny name for a dog. And the wife pokes herself with her finger and laughs. These examples clearly demonstrate that the drover's wife is funny.

On the other hand, sadness. There are several very tragic parts of the book such as when the wife cries after touching the blackfellow's wood. And when she is missing her drover, who is far away in Ireland. And also when there was a flood and a bushfire and the snake. But at the end after killing the snake, the drover's wife has a cuddle with her son and feels better, so it is not all sad.

In conclusion, the drover's wife in 'The Drover's Wife' is well portrayed by flashbacks, description, humour and sadness, and marks Henry Lawson as one of the greatest living Australian writers.

List of Ingredients

INGREDIENTS: Bush starch (78%), Snake Oil (Black), Alligator steak, Aqua (rainwater), Tabasco 'Bushfire' Sauce (551), Bullock's Testicles, Chicken Stock, Crow, Fried Snake Flavour (E309), Colouring 422 (Sickly Daylight).

Store in a hot, dry place.

Made in Australia.

Warning: Products packaged after 1970 may contain traces of metafiction.

A Cryptic Crossword

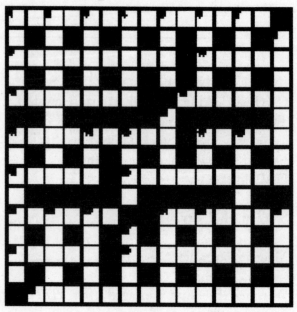

ACROSS

1   She wrote fervid, moving short story (3,7,4)

9   Agent and flyboys get blokes who fix things (9)

10 Pointy version of 26-down? (5)

11 Rough time after beginning drinking dry spell (7)

12 Merchant sends back Russian paintings (6)

13 Partner's wandering bush and. . . (7)

14 Family wearing tights back to front leaves
    nothing to the imagination? (4-5)

17, 28 Dangerous creature to nibble Romantic
        poet, according to Spooner (5,5)

19   British soldier's rock opera (5)

20   Reporters ruffled her conman (9)

21   Historical feast? (6)

24   According to Henry Lawson's contemporary, he camped in a billabong (7)

28   See 17-across

29   Wild gorilla at large (animal they cannot afford to lose) (9)

30   Investigation of buyers shifting hectare markers (6,8)

DOWN

1   Loveless editor irritated and worn out (5)

2   Heard phoney hesitation supporting EU instrument (9)

3   Lamenting bankruptcy then ultimately droving (5)

4   *Sick Hearts* – novel for Winton's comeback (5)

5   Moorhouse's cutting opening line (4)

6   After change of heart, bet there's almost none of it in the creek? (5)

7   Disaster as weevil tail found in food (5)

8   1-across remains so poor during nun's upset (8)

13   Notice missing skin of the ear? (4)

14   Perhaps Ryan O'Neill's art is silly . . . it's funny? (8)

15   Essay, poetry, prose regularly ignored (3)

16   Content featured in *Young Ladies' Journal* (4)

17   Born 17 June 1867 in Grenfell, Albion *[some of that shouldn't be there]* (3)

18   Old school mother surrounded by change (4,5)

22   Climbing mountain with zeal oddly leads to shopping centre? (5)

23   Prowl and shake 28-across (5)

24   Al and Victor invested in snakeskin oil? (5)

25   Glean new perspective (5)

26   Pointy version of 10-across? (5)

27   *[Need sickly daylight at the end]* (4)

Crossword by Christopher Black, with Ryan O'Neill

Cryptic Crossword Answers

ACROSS

1 She wrote fervid, moving [anagram indicator] **short story** (3,7,4) = THE DROVER'S WIFE

9 Agent [REP] and flyboys [AIRMEN] get **blokes who fix things** (9) = REPAIRMEN

10 **Pointy** version of [anagram indicator] 26-down? (5) = THORN [this is not a usual cryptic clue as the cross-reference is circular, and the definition is just a description, a thorn is pointy]

11 Rough time [T] after beginning [D] rinking **dry spell** (7) = DROUGHT

12 **Merchant** sends back [reversal indicator] Russian [RED] paintings [ART] (6) = TRADER

13 **Partner**'s wandering [anagram indicator] bush and . . . (7) = HUSBAND [As you might have noticed, there is no 13-across, it's an absent husband.]

14 Family [KIN] wearing [contained by] tights back to front [STIGHT] **leaves nothing to the imagination?** (4-5) = SKIN-TIGHT

17, 28 **Dangerous creature** to nibble [SNACK] Romantic poet [BLAKE], according to Spooner [Spoonerism, swap initial sounds of the two words] (5,5) = BLACK SNAKE

19 **British soldier**'s [two definitions] **rock opera** (5) = TOMMY

20 **Reporters** ruffled [anagram indicator]

her conman (9) = ANCHORMEN

21 Historical [a cryptic pun, re (as in
concerning) past] **feast**? (6) = REPAST

24 According to Henry Lawson's contemporary,
he camped in a billabong (7) = SWAGMAN
[just a straight clue, but written to sound
like the contemporary (Banjo Paterson)
is talking about Lawson rather than the
swagman from 'Waltzing Matilda'.]

29 Wild [anagram indicator] gorilla at **large (animal
they cannot afford to lose)** (9) = ALLIGATOR

30 **Investigation of buyers** shifting [anagram indicator]
hectare markers (6,8) = MARKET RESEARCH

DOWN

1 Loveless [Lacking love, which as in tennis is O] editor
irritated [anagram indicator] and **worn out** (5) = TIRED

2 Heard [homophone indicator] phoney
hesitation [UM] supporting [appearing below]
EU **instrument** (9) = EUPHONIUM

3 **Lamenting** bankruptcy [RUIN] then ultimately
[last, or ultimate, letter] drovin[G] (5) = RUING

4 *Sick Hearts* [hearts, or central letters] –
no[V]el f[O]r Winton's [TIM] comeback
[reversal indicator] (5) = VOMIT

5 Moorhouse's [FRANK] cutting opening
[losing first letter] **line** (4) = RANK

6 After change of heart [change centre
letter], bet [WAGER] **there's almost none
of it in the creek**? (5) = WATER

7 **Disaster** as weevi[L] tail [last letter] found in
[container indicator] food (5) = FLOOD

8 **1-across remains so** poor during
nun's upset (8) = UNBROKEN

13 Notice missing skin **of the ear**? (4) = OTIC

14 **Perhaps Ryan O'Neill's** art is silly [anagram indicator]
. . . it's funny [anagram indicator]? (8) = SATIRIST

15 **Essay**, poetry, prose regularly [even letters=POE]
ignored [removed, i.e. poetry] (3) = TRY

16 **Content** featured in [hidden indicator]

Young Ladies' Journal (4) = GLAD

17 Born 17 June 1867 in Grenfell, Albion *[some of that shouldn't be there]* (3) = BIO ['some of that shouldn't be there' indicates the hidden clue and the answer as a whole, the start is largely Henry Lawson's actual bio, the 'Albion' shouldn't be there.]

18 **Old school** mother surrounded by change (4,5) = ALMA MATER

22 Climbing mountain with zeal oddly leads to **shopping centre**? (5) = PLAZA

23 **Prowl** and shake [anagram indicator] 28-across (5) = SNEAK

24 Al and Victor [V] invested in [container indicator] snakeskin [S_E] **oil**? (5) = SALVE

25 Glean new [anagram indicator] **perspective** (5) = ANGLE

26 **Pointy** version of [anagram indicator] 10-across? (5) = NORTH [this is not a usual cryptic clue as the cross-reference is circular, and the definition is just a description, north is pointy, like a compass point]

27 *[**Need** sickly [WAN] dayligh[T] at the end]* (4) = WANT

A Child's Drawing

An Agony Aunt Column

Does he love you, or does he love ewe?

Dear Pamela,

My husband is a drover, and his work frequently takes him away from home for months on end, leaving me to look after our four young children. Sometimes I get so lonely I could have a good cry. Last week, while my husband was absent yet again, a black snake came into the house, terrifying the children and myself before I managed to kill it. I love my husband, but I don't know how much longer I can stand this solitary lifestyle. In the last five years there have been fires, floods and mad bulls to contend with. I'm at my wit's end. Please tell me what I should do.

—The Drover's Wife

Dear Drover's Wife,

Quite simply, your husband has to choose between you and ewes. I know many people are doing it tough at the moment, but I don't believe for one second that an able-bodied man can't find work closer to home. You have been left on your own so much, you are in danger of losing your sense of identity. It concerns me deeply that you signed your letter 'The Drover's Wife', which indicates that this is how you define yourself. You are so much more than a wife to a largely absent man. You are a mother, a lover, and a warrior. You are a woman, and never forget that. Don't be a sheep. Your husband sees enough of those at work.

A snake drove Adam and Eve apart, but it may be the cause of bringing you and your husband together. Send him a telegram tonight and tell him how frightened you were when you saw the snake, and how much you needed him. Men like to feel they are protecting their family, and I have a suspicion this will release something primal in your husband, and he will come running home. Just remember not to gush or make a fuss when he does.

—Pamela

Sporting Commentary

The Drover's Wife
vs. The Black Snake

A: Good afternoon everyone, and welcome to Lawson Arena for what promises to be a night of high drama. Isn't that right, Gary?

B: It certainly is, Steve. The tension could, quite literally, be cut with a knife. It's not every day you see a match of this calibre: the Drover's Wife against the Black Snake.

A: On paper, the Black Snake is the one to beat. Two and a half metres long, it's Australia's largest venomous reptile. Granted, he's never been known to kill an adult, but there's a lot at stake tonight and this game might rewrite the history books.

B: Obviously, at the end of the day, you're 100% correct, Steve-o. The stats do lean in the Black Snake's favour, but bear in mind the Drover's Wife is fielding six players.

A: Four of those are, in fact, children, which the Black Snake has, in fact, been known to kill. That has got to be on the mind of the captain tonight.

B: That's not all that'll be on her mind tonight. With the Drover playing an away game—

A: Sorry to interrupt you there, Gary, but there's movement on the field. And what a field it is. Bush all around – bush with no horizon. The country is flat. No undergrowth. Perfect playing conditions and a real tribute to the groundskeepers.

B: It appears . . . yes! The players have assembled in standard formation, while the captain, the Drover's Wife, oversees from the kitchen. Classic. And is this a challenge already? Yes! Here he comes—

A: The Black Snake! He's moving forward quickly, not wasting any time. Look at him go, menacing the defence. Number 3, that's little Tommy, is calling for the captain.

B: And here she comes! Steve, would you just listen to that crowd?

A: The Drover's Wife isn't mucking about. She's reaching for a club. A nice green sapling. Excellent choice. Little Tommy is crouching in reserve . . . The snake is . . . Hold on—

B: It's Alligator on the attack! What a great move!

He's all over the Black Snake like a rash. Would you just look at that tackle!

A: Great effort there from the dog. He'll be having some pig ears tonight for a treat, no doubt. If he survives, that is.

B: The crowd are on their feet. They think it's all over!

A: I wouldn't be betting against the snake just yet. He wasn't born yesterday.

B: Here's Little Tommy in support. He's lifting his club. It looks like his timing is off—

A: Can you believe it?! He's brought it down on Alligator instead. What a shambles. The snake's gotten away. He's under the house. He's clear!

B: You've got to give the snake credit for that, don't you, Steve?

A: You've got to, Gary. The Drover's Wife looks mighty disappointed with Tommy and who can blame her? Now she's pulling the whole team inside. Little Tommy is protesting, but she's not having a bar of it.

B: This is one for the books. And while we await the next exciting development in the match, let's hear a word from our sponsors.

Woman: Come on, darling! It's three o'clock. Time to visit my mother.

Man: Fair dinkum!

Woman: And after that you promised you'd go clothes shopping with me, remember?

Man: Strewth!

Woman: Then there's dinner with Linda and Gary, my two vegan friends, from England. I'm sure you'll have lots to talk about.

Man: My oath! It's going to take nerves of steel to get through today. I need a Steelman's! [Glug, glug, glug]

Woman: Are you ready, darling?

Man: Ready? The footy's on, and there's a slab of Steelman's in the fridge. I'm not going anywhere.

Woman: But what about mum, and the shopping, and Linda and Gary?

Man: Well then, darl, you had better steel yourself for a disappointment. Now get me another beer!

Woman: Oh, Norm! [giggles]

Voiceover: Remember, women want a real man, and that means a Steelman. Drink Steelman's.

A: I don't know about you, Gary, but when I'm watching sport there's nothing I like better than a nice cold Steelman's.

B: Me too, Steve-o. And speaking of steel, here she comes, the woman of steel. Let's not forget what she's capable of. This is the woman who last year single-handedly murdered the Bullocks—

A: She gave The Crows a good hiding too. Not so convincing against the Adelaide Swagmen, but you can't win 'em all.

B: She'll give it a red hot go though, and there she is, back on the field. She's brought Alligator, but not the children. That's a wise move, especially since the wet weather's closed in. What is that she's reading, Steve? *Sports Illustrated*?

A: From this angle it looks like the *Young Ladies' Journal*, Gary. Look out! She's giving it everything she's got. One hundred and ten per cent.

B: Well she'll need to stay focused. The Black Snake's a character who can't be underestimated.

A: It's anyone's game and the clock is running down. Someone's got to act and my guess is it'll be the snake to step things up to the next level. He better not leave it too long – the crowd won't be happy with a draw tonight.

B: You mean this morning, Steve. The sun will be up in a few minutes, and with it the referee's whistle. I think this . . . Wait . . . Yes. Yes! It's the snake! He's coming out from under the floor!

A: Just look at that dog bristle. Just look at him!

B: The snake is advancing. He's advancing. But Alligator and the Drover's Wife are not messing around. They're up. They're up. And they're on him!

A: Teamwork!

B: This is do or die but the dog's got the snake! And here comes the stick!

A: That snake is on fire!

B: He's giving it all he's got.

A: No, he is literally on fire! The snake is in the fire, and the crowd are on their feet! The Drover's Wife has won!

B: Here comes Tommy! He's celebrating with his captain and rightly so. What do you think he's saying, Steve-o?

A: I can't be sure, but emotions are obviously running high. What a tremendous sight.

B: It sure is. The best team won.

A: It certainly did, Gary. It certainly did. Well folks, that's all from Lawson Arena. Please join us next Sunday for what promises to be the grudge match to end all grudge matches – that's Squeaker versus his Mate. Don't miss it!

A Disease

Drover's Wife Disease (DWD) is an infectious pathogenic bacteria found most commonly in isolated bush areas around Hungerford and Bourke, NSW. Women with multiple children, who have spent significant amounts of time alone, are most vulnerable to this disease. Men over the age of sixteen are immune to DWD, but can be infected by its mutated variant, Joe Wilson Syndrome (JWS).

Transmission
DWD is spread by red-bellied black snakes. The disease can be transmitted through a bite, but also by being in close physical proximity to the snake for more than a few seconds.

Symptoms
The patient will initially feel hyper-active and inclined to physical movement, such as picking up wooden clubs, or running vigorously around the garden. However, due to the cyclic lifestyle of the bacteria, as soon as night falls the patient is likely to feel lethargic and depressed. A high fever (the 'bushfire' phase) is then followed by copious sweating

(the 'downpour' phase). This can be succeeded by hallucinatory flashbacks, and occasionally an outbreak of distressingly racist language, usually directed at Indigenous people. The next stage is marked by insomnia and paranoia, and it is not unusual for the patient to believe that the snake who transmitted the infection is lurking nearby. Speech centres may also be affected, hence the alternative name for DWD, 'Bung Syndrome.' The terminal stage of the disease is characterised by violent behaviour, such as beating at the imaginary snake, and emotional outbursts, including pathological nostalgia and weeping fits. Without treatment, the patient invariably expires shortly after sunrise.

Treatment

Four rotten native apples and six figs of tobacco taken orally twice a day retards the growth of the bacteria, and eventually destroys it. Anecdotal evidence suggests reading to the patient from the *Young Ladies' Journal* may have a calming effect. In chronic cases, it is recommended that a male relative – preferably a husband – should remain in attendance.

Outlook

For patients who receive proper and prompt treatment, the morbidity rate stands at 29.34%. More information can be found in:

Baynton, B. (1902) Several observations regarding Drover's Wife Disease. *Bush Studies*, 41(2), 143-151.

Lipogram

A bush cabin in an outlying part of Australia marks a distant location for our story. Horizon cut off by mountains; shrubs and saplings all around. Two small boys and two young girls play out front on a straggly lawn. (At this point I should say that missing from my account is a man, daddy to this group of kids. Also AWOL is a solitary sign. A hint for unmindful bookworms – it's not a consonant.) Anyway, a long animal slinks from within a patch of grass. (It's not a boa, or an anaconda or an asp, or a mamba. But it's similar in many ways in that it's without limbs, it slinks, and is poisonous, and has cold blood. Not only that, this thing's occasionally a synonym for 'bastard.' In short, it's a noxious varmint.)

'Ma, Ma!' Jacky starts to call. 'Quick. It's a snak–!' but his warning is cut off by it moving towards him. A woman runs out and grabs a stick, as Alligator (a trusty hound, not a croc, I must clarify now, to avoid confusion) attacks this black animal, growling at it. Aghast, it worms its way down into a crack in a stringybark slab.

Night. Our family sits indoors, gulping down a hasty bit of grub. Soon, all but a solitary lady is unconscious. Hank Lawson, original author of this work, didn't allow his daunting matron an alias. I say this is laxity on his part, and so I shall, from now on, call our valiant protagonist, Marian. Any opposition to my accord? Too bad. Moving on now.

As Alligator naps on a dirty patch of floor, Marian sits and thinks about days past. Conflagrations, floods, starving crows, angry bullocks, and a rapacious swagman. All of this is brought to mind during a long, still, forlorn night. Soon, it's past four o'clock. Not long until daylight, and it's hot from wood burning in a hob. Without warning, Alligator snarls at an approaching, shadowy form. Marian grasps a trusty club and stands by. No sound but a bloodcurdling hiss. Thud, thud! Stick and tooth attack, and in an instant a scaly thing is stiff and cold.

Haggard, drawn, Marian falls into a faint, worn out by combat and worry. Tiny Tommy, with filial alacrity, runs out and Marian hugs him.

'Ma, I won't do dad's job. Blarst it, I won't!'

Woman and son sit thus as sickly daylight glints across a bush background.

Freudian

The motif of the children at play is an indication that the writer wishes to return to some aspect of his youth. The approaching snake may signify that a problem is worrying the writer, but it more likely symbolises the male genitalia in its flaccid state. The dog is a symbol of the writer's animalistic nature. (Note how this nature is first chained up (repressed) but quickly becomes too strong and escapes its bonds.) The snake penetrating deep under the house is, it need hardly be said, a representation of sexual intercourse. The floods that the main character recalls represent female sexual arousal, and the bushfires are analogous to sexual passion, while the drought expresses a deep-seated anxiety of the results of this passion. The woman beating the snake is a blatant symbol of castration (or, alternatively, masturbation) while the snake being thrown on the fire demonstrates the writer's fear of impotence; note how the snake shrivels into nothing. The sunrise at the end of the story suggests the beginning of a new story: a period of refreshment and renewal for the writer.

Or, more probably, it represents a penis.

A Mixtape

1. *World Down Under* by Ace of Base

2. *Beating Around the Bush* by AC/DC

3. *In a Lonely Place* by New Order

4. *Along Comes a Woman* by Chicago

5. *Let the Children Play* by Santana

6. *A Young Man is Gone* by The Beach Boys

7. *Snake in the Grass* by Jed Hughes

8. *Alligator Mine* by Arcade Fire

9. *Rolling Thunder* by A-Ha

10. *Gimme Shelter* by The Rolling Stones

11. *Children's Lullaby* by Vertical Horizon

12. *Woman Tonight* by America

13. *I Can't Go to Sleep* by the Wu Tang Clan

14. *Separation Anxiety* by American Hi-Fi

15. *Do You Remember the Time* by Amy Grant

16. *Every Woman Dreams* by Shanice Wilson

17. *Lost in the Flood* by Bruce Springsteen

18. *Wildfire* by P.O.D.

19. *Story about a Man with a Bad Heart* by Emery

20. *Even Now* by Bob Seger

21. *Laugh & Cry* by Chuck Berry

22. *Danger* by Hilary Duff

23. *Snake Fighter* by 3 Inches of Blood

24. *Fire Snakes* by Laura Veirs

25. *Morning has Broken* by Cat Stevens

26. *Mother and Son* by Star Barefoot Walker

A 1950s Children's Book

There was once a bush farm that the sun rose over,
And on that little farm lived the wife of a drover.
The drover (her husband) was away with his sheep.
(He was a more masculine version of Little Bo-Peep.)

So with just the wife, and four children only,
It has to be said she sometimes felt lonely.
(I mustn't forget the mutt, Alligator,
But never mind now, there's time for that later.)

Bush to the left, bush to the right,
Bush stretching on, far out of sight.
Nothing but earth, trees, dirt and mud,
With seasonal bushfires and occasional flood.

Now not far away from the house of the drover,
Half asleep in the sun without any cover,
As long and thin and straight as a rake
Was a friendly black reptile called Cecil Snake.

Cecil was sad, and felt just a touch isolated,
So towards the modest shack he undulated.

Then hearing children at play, he went even faster,
Little thinking he headed for certain disaster.

A tall, thin figure loomed up on his right,
And since Cecil was told to be always polite,
On seeing the wife, he said 'How'd you do, Miss?'
But all she could hear was a terrible hiss.

Cecil reared up to give her a bow,
Oh, you've never heard such a terrible row!
Pity poor Cecil, the cause of this strife.
'Snake!' screamed the woman, 'Run for your life!'

As the woman and children fast disappeared,
Cecil heard a growl and became much afeared.
The snake was never a cat or dog hater
But he didn't take to that hound, Alligator.

A battle? Hardly! More like a rout
With Cecil fleeing before the great snout
Of the hound and quickly under the house
Where he lay silent and scared as a mouse.

'Why did that happen? Was it something I did?'
Panicky thoughts filled him as he hid.
'I'm an innocent snake, not bad like some adders,
I just wanted a game of Snakes and Ladders.'

All the long night, he lay there so cold
But when the dawn came, he began to feel bold.
'I'll make friends with that human, see if I'm right!'
And so he slithered into the light.

'Dear lady, forgive me,' Cecil did hiss.
'I'm sorry that things have gone so amiss.
You're lonely, I'm lonely, so let's be mates.
A glorious friendship between us awaits!'

'Would you be so kind as to call off your dog?
As you see I'm not moving, as still as a log.'
Then Cecil saw, (and it made him quite sick)
The wife of the drover reach for a stick.

Poor Cecil pulled such hideous faces
While his back was busted in several places.
Thus, he closed his eyes and thought 'Such is life'
As he was done to death by the drover's wife.

What funeral was there, what mourning and prayer?
None! Unfortunate Cecil was thrown in the air,
Tumbling and falling in widening gyre
His reptilian corpse cast into the fire.

Far, far away, twenty miles at a run
Cecil's wife holds close their little son.
'Dad's home soon, baby. Don't cry now, shoosh.'
While sickly daylight breaks over the bush.

McCarthyesque

The adobe house lay like some ill begotten Argonaut
lost in the purlieu of an antique country. In front of it a
galimaufry of striplings were serried asquint in the long
wallowed afternoon. Their clamour hushed and con-
gruent amidst the lucent diorama of environs scurvid
and sere.

Madre, the boy said.

Yes?

The woman emerged from the dimness of the
house. Her calico dress bedight with great chevrons of
light which the boy adduced to the chamfer of veranda
post and roof.

Hay una serpiente negra en el jardín.

Qué dijiste.

Por ahí. Mira.

The boy indicated the ferric earth and the serpent
upon it carven from a caul of darkness unhurriedly
progressing across the chaparral. Eyes chary with some
unknowable consciousness. Legatee of the arrant and
deadly as any vinegarroon.

Si. Si, lo veo, the woman said. *Ven aqui.*

Why?

Ven aquí. Ahora.

Without haste the boy went to her like some reluctant marionette importuned by an egregious master. The woman dandled the babies to her breast and took a stick in her hand. Then looked the snake up and down and after a moment went towards it. At that instant the dog came howling out of its kennel like some damned soul unfettered from the bajadas of hell. The black and ancient snake was lost under the house.

Inside, the woman said.

They ate dinner. The two boys were talking.

Me está pelando vivo con su palo

Si te muerden, te hinchas y hueles y te vuelves rojo y verde y azul hasta que mueras

Si, si, said the younger boy.

You be quiet now, the woman said. After a while they went to sleep.

The thunder cataclysmed over the darkling plain like some tatterdemalion lunatic discalced in a serried suit of fire and rain drubbed the lone shack in the gibbous moonlight. A debouched prophesy of brimstone and judgement on the woman as she sat awaiting the laggard serpent. Her long hair plaited and her adorned in nothing but a sark. Heart genuflecting like some predacious acolyte before a bloodied altar lost to the memory of the earth.

The benighted house was quiet as the woman perused the *Young Ladies' Journal*. At her feet the dog slept. After a time she had an augury of her decamped husband climbing up through a ratchel of eucalyptus and rotten native apple trees. His whip in hand to quirt the rimpled creatures ahead of him. Then she envisioned dreams ensephulcred in the sacristy of her memory. A phantasmagoria of truculent infernos suzerain over the swale and whinstone. Extemporary parlays with plug hatted importunate swagmen well cognisant of her husband's temporal elision. Inimical buzzards chary of her broomstick, wheeling in a sky white as sclera.

When the visions had passed the woman sat for a long time before she got up and went outside to fetch some wood. The moon hung like a cataracted eye over the rim of the world. She went back inside and sat down, warming her hands by the fire. When at last the serpent egressed she accoutred herself with the stick. By her the dog, acolyte bipartisan and atavism incarnate. The snake defiled between them and analogue to some heathen berserker she clubbed it as the canine seized it by the tail. Then she threw the snake in the fire.

The boy stood beside her, a grubby noctambulist.

No te dejaré nunca. Maldita sea si lo hago, he said.

She took him in her arms. And watched as the sanguinolent sun broke over the cordillera.

Parable

Matthew Chapter 24

¹ And Jesus went down to the lake of Galilee, and there a multitude formed about him to listen to his words.

² And so he told unto them a parable, saying:

³ Hearken; Behold, there went out a drover to drive his sheep:

⁴ And it came to pass, as he drove his sheep, his wife and children were left alone.

⁵ And one day, a snake did come about them.

⁶ The woman and the children hid themselves from the snake.

⁷ But later the woman caught the snake, and burnt it.

⁸ And when Jesus was alone, one of the twelve asked of him the parable.

⁹ And he said unto them, He that hath ears to hear, let him hear.

¹⁰ The kingdom of heaven is likened unto the wife of the drover.

¹¹ He that destroyeth the serpent shall inherit the kingdom prepared for them from the foundation of the world.

¹² But he that is away when evil is abroad shall be cast into outer darkness, where there is no daylight, not even that which is sickly.

¹³ And there shall be weeping and gnashing of teeth.

Editorial Comments

1. Henry, I know we have discussed this before, but I'm still not sold on the title. How about 'Snake!' or 'A Bush Adventure'?

2. Present tense is a little overused nowadays. Would you consider changing to past?

3. 'The drover, an ex-squatter, is away with sheep. His wife and children are left here alone.' As in this example, you do 'tell' quite a lot in this story, rather than 'show'. Please consider revising.

4. I see that you still haven't given the drover or his wife a name. I think the story would work much better if the characters were named. How about Phil and Natasha?

5. I still maintain 'Crocodile' would be a better name for the dog. Alligators aren't found in Australia, after all.

6. As per a previous comment. Only two of the children have names; Tommy and Jacky. Name the other two.

7. The *Young Ladies' Journal* is published by a rival firm. Change this to *Australian Women's Weekly*?

8. I know you're squeamish when it comes to swear words, but it is difficult to shock a reader nowadays. Instead of '(adjective) possums', have a think about 'sodding possums' or 'fucking/motherfucking possums'. It hasn't hurt Christos Tsiolkas, has it?

9. 'No use fretting' is a good line, but a little stilted and old fashioned. A simple 'No worries' would work better.

10. You mention a brother-in-law here. Perhaps Natasha is having a torrid affair with him? Just a thought.

11. Henry: I know you aren't racist, but 'blackman,' 'blackfellow' and 'Black Mary' could certainly be interpreted as such, especially as these characters are very much more 'flat' than 'round'. Please read the article I sent you last week, 'Creating Believable Aboriginal and Torres Strait Islander Characters'.

12. I'm bothered about the cruelty to animals you portray in these paragraphs. Does the bullock have to die? Perhaps he is not mad and merely hungry. This would give us a chance to see a more sympathetic side of the wife. Also, these scenes might land us in trouble with PETA types. Revise?

13. Instead of a swagman, perhaps a rather pretty swagwoman might appear? This is an interesting twist, and could lead to an intriguing new direction for the story. Think how successful *Brokeback Mountain* was!

14. As I mentioned above, I have reservations about the lazy 'blackfellow' here. It won't be a problem, of course, if you intend to submit only to *Quadrant*.

15. Ha-ha! I love the holey handkerchief. In fact, I think the story could benefit from more humour of this kind.

16. Perhaps instead of burning the snake, she could make a belt of it? I like the symbolism of this.

17. The last line: consider deleting.

A Children's Toy

Say G'Day to New Drover's Wife™ Barbie®!

Girls of all ages who dream of living a rugged life in the Australian outback will love new Drover's Wife™ Barbie®. Sporting an elegant sunfaded gingham dress with six individually sewn buttons and a pair of kangaroo skin moccasins, Barbie® is ready to face any fair dinkum challenge the outback throws at her. Featuring pushmove™®© technology: press a button on Barbie's® back and watch her beat a snake to death!

Includes: loveable frisky cocker spaniel 'Alligator,' ® a wooden club and makeup kit.

Barbie® Drover's Wife™ Bush Shanty and solarium, Barbie Drover's Wife™ Tommy, Barbie Drover's Wife™ Jacky and Barbie Drover's Wife™ 8 cm long red-bellied black snake not included.

Ken® as The Drover™ currently unavailable.

Doll cannot stand alone as shown.

Elizabethan

The Merry Wife of Drover

PROLOGUE

Enter Chorus

CHORUS

A household, poor but rich in dignity
In fair Australia where we lay our scene
Bush all around it stretches to infinity
No indoor plumbing, just an old latrine.
The two-roomed house is built of timber slats.
A wife and children live here all alone,
The husband's gone among the endless flats,
A droving with his sheep in lands unknown.
Now is the summer of her discontent
Made glorious legend by this Austral play,
And so the endless days of her torment
Shall give the stuff to make dramatic clay.
Look upon her with your welkin eye: God sake!
And pray for her when she doth meet the snake!

[Exit

ACT 1, SCENE 1

Outside a rustic hut in the Antipodean desert.

Enter JACKY and TOMMY

JACKY

> Nine changes of the watery star hath been
> The shepherd's note since father left our house.

TOMMY

> I am questioned by my fears of what may chance
> Or breed upon his absence, look you now
> Nineteen long miles from other men are we,
> From heartiness, from bounty, and from life.

Enter a SNAKE.

JACKY

> Peace, break thee off; look, there it comes, a
>   snake!

TOMMY

> A snake! A snake! Help mother, here's a snake!

Enter THE DROVER'S WIFE and ALLIGATOR.

THE DROVER'S WIFE

> False serpent that didst flatter mother Eve,
> I'll fetch a stick and cudgel out its brains!

All four chase the SNAKE around the stage.

[Exeunt SNAKE, pursued by JACKY, TOMMY and ALLI-GATOR.

THE DROVER'S WIFE

> Thy tongue outvenoms all the worms of Nile.
> A corse I'll make of thee, thou monster vile!

[Exit

ACT 1, SCENE 2

A room inside the hut.

Enter THE DROVER'S WIFE and ALLIGATOR

THE DROVER'S WIFE
>The children are a-bed now, let them sleep
>Till morn appears to light this dateless night.
>Behold! The sky is dropping fire, and the great
>Dark firmament is ripp'd by thunder stones.
>Good things of day begin to droop and drowse,
>Whilst night's black agents to their preys do
>>rouse.

She crosses the stage.

>Methought I heard a voice hiss, 'Sleep no more!'
>It is the damn'ed snake has murdered sleep.
>I must awake, and factious be, lest the
>Enchafed black serpent get the start of me.
>Fie! Mine is but a dormouse valour, which
>Shall never stay but scurry in the dark.

She examines a locket around her neck.

THE DROVER'S WIFE
>As I do live, my husband, where art thou?
>Encaved in meadow with the sheep or worse
>Than that, a drabbing with the city whores?
>Alone I am, and drops of sorrow cascade
>Their silver ways beneath my red-rimmed eyes.
>Four kiddies and a dog, and a worn out goodwife.
>No cater-cousins nor a Christian soul
>And no use fretting.

ALLIGATOR
>Woof, woof! Woof woof!
>Woof, woof, woof, woof, woof woof!

THE DROVER'S WIFE

> I am undone: there is no living, none,
> If Drover be away. 'Twere all one
> That I should love a bright particular star
> And think to wed it, he is so above me:
> In his bright radiance and collateral light
> Must I be comforted, not in his sphere.
> But now he's gone, and my idolatrous fancy
> Must sanctify his reliques.

A sound of thunder.

THE DROVER'S WIFE

> The rain outside is like to turn this place
> Into an ark. The *Journal of Young Ladies*,
> Preserve my wits. Now fashion plates I'll see.
> Oh, would that I could sleep, I'd dream of him!
> My Alligator, I do envy thee
> Thy peace. Too little have I known of it.
> One baby dead, and others sick and still
> Some others full of pith and cool offence.
> The dam across the creek will crack no doubt.
> Or conflagrations cross this cursed place
> Like to the scars across a whipped slave's back.
> Yet 'twill keep the carrion crows off
> And a man's life's no more than to say 'Bung.'
> Would I were with him! He would always say—
>   Methinks I hear him now; his plausive words
> 'I do love nothing in the world so well as you: is
> not that strange?'
> O proper stuff! Damn this occulted snake!

Enter SNAKE

THE DROVER'S WIFE

> Soft, what hiss through yonder corner breaks?
> Pale Hecate's curse, it is the serpent!
> A stick! A stick! My kingdom for a stick!

THE DROVER'S WIFE and the SNAKE fight. The SNAKE is beaten by THE DROVER'S WIFE and thrown upon the fire.

THE DROVER'S WIFE

>Now cracks a noble heart.–Good night, sweet
>>snake
>And flights of emus sing thee to thy rest!
>
>[Aside:] He was a snake, take him for all and all.
>I shall not look upon his like again.

Enter TOMMY

TOMMY

>Alas! A drover will I never be, I swear't.

THE DROVER'S WIFE

>But, look, the morn, in russet mantle clad,
>Walks o'er the dew of yon high eastward hill
>And heaven's eye shines sickly over all.

[Exeunt

Lecture Slides

Henry Lawson (1867-1922)

- Mother Louisa: Publisher, poet, feminist
- Father Niels Larsen (Lawson): Miner
- Education: Dickens, Harte, Marryat, Poe, Clarke.
- Deafness
- Early Writings: Poetry
- Time in the bush: Hungerford to Bourke, 1892
- The Bulletin Debate: Paterson's romanticism vs Lawson's realism

Henry Lawson (1867-1922)

- Short Story Collection *While the Billy Boils* published in 1896 (includes 'The Drover's Wife.')
- Miserable Marriage
- Later Writings (Joe Mitchell)
- Alcoholism
- Death

The Drover's Wife

The Drover's Wife: Style

- Documentary
- 'Realist' (cf. Ada Cambridge, Barbara Baynton)
- Sketch vs Short Story
- Description of Bush
- Dialogue: Colloquial

The Drover's Wife: Themes

- The Bush: Threatening, lonely, hostile, sickly, hard, hot, muddy, dirty, wet.
- Love (Unsentimental)
- Bravery
- Stoicism/Fatalism

The Drover's Wife: Characters

- The Drover: Ex-squatter, six months away, 'careless, but a good enough husband.' Generous. Unfaithful? 'An Australian.'
- The Drover's Wife: 'Gaunt, sunbrowned.' Five Children (One dead). Contemplative, taciturn. Interested in Fashion. Retains a sense of the ridiculous.
- Alligator: 'Dog-of-all-breeds.' Ugly, scarred, unafraid, a 'snake-dog.'
- The Snake: Black, 'Evil,' Five feet long.

Problematic depiction of Indigenous Characters

* King Jimmy
* Black Mary: 'the "whitest" gin in all the land'
* "A stray blackfellow... the last of his tribe and a King; but he had built that wood-heap hollow"

The Drover's Wife: Symbolism

* The Drover
* The Drover's Wife
* The Snake
* The Bush

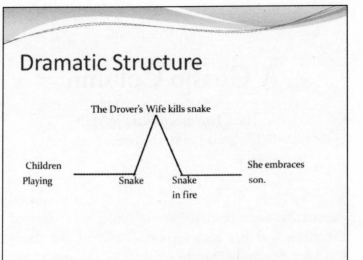

The Drover's Wife: Legacy

- 'On Our Selection' by Steele Rudd (1905)
- '...the dreary dun-coloured offspring of journalistic realism.' Patrick White
- 'The Drover's Wife' by Russell Drysdale (1945)
- 'The Drover's Wife' by Murray Bail (1975)
- 'The Drover's Wife' by Barbara Jefferis (1980)
- 'The Drover's Wife' by Frank Moorhouse (1980)
- 'The Drover's Wife' by Mandy Sayer (1996)
- 'The Drover's Wife' by Leah Purcell (2016)
- 'The Drover's Wife' by Frank Moorhouse (Ed.) (2017)

A Gossip Column

The Drover and his Wife
'still crazy in love.'

Australia's sweetheart, the drover's wife, has confirmed that she and her husband are still 'head over heels in love' despite her not being seen on the arm of the hunky squatter for the last six months. Sources close to the couple say the drover's wife is perfectly happy spending quality time with her four children and her labradoodle, Alligator, at the showbiz couple's luxurious stringybark bush retreat. 'She loves it out there,' 'Mary,' a close personal friend revealed, 'but that's not to say that there haven't been tough times.' Certainly few could forget the photographs of the drover's wife which surfaced last year in the *Young Ladies' Journal*, unbowed by the bushfires raging around her estate. And fewer still would forget the price she charged for the snaps, rumoured to be in six figures.

Yet even this is thought to be small potatoes compared with the sums that HarperCollins paid the drover's wife for her memoir, which gives an account of her battles with depression and PTSD brought about by an encounter with a rabid cow several years ago. And, as our source 'Mary' exclusively reveals, another book might be on the way. 'Just last week she told me she had a sleepless night when a black snake came into the house. Only her belief in the Kabbalah, and a big stick got her through it.' That certainly won't be the last we hear of this incident, especially if the reality TV show that has been on the cards for the last few years finally gains some traction.

Meanwhile, the drover maintains that he and Edith Campbell-Berry are 'just good friends.'

Glaswegian

The hen and her weans bide in a wee but an ben far awa' frae 'er neighboors. There's big trees aw aroond them an' a wee creek runnin' pest. 'Er guidman is a gallus cheil. E's a drover an' has bin awa' fur ages, so she's aft crabbit. A body day, a snake appears, an' th' dug goes fuckin' mental.

'Away tae fuck!' th' drover's guidwife sez an she gits a chib tae belt th' snake. 'Mon then!' she sez, then aw th' fowk hae tae rin inside.

They hae tatties an' neeps fur tea, an' then they gab fur a lang time. Thocht th' weans don't wantae gang tae sleep, the drover's guidwife sez she'll gie them a skelp an she maks them. Ootside, it starts tae pish doon. Th' guidwife decides tae sit up aw nicht an' watch fur th' snake. She thinks abit aw th' things she's seen, th' fires an' floods, an' 'er guidman. She's hud a lonely life, a pure nigel nae pals so she wiz, but she doesnae ken anither. In th' past, she's hud tae barnie radge bulls, crows an' aw kinds o diseases.

'Dinnae fash yersel,' she is aye sayin' as there's fuck all she can dae aboot it.

Sometimes a blooter'd dobber ur sum ither fuckin' shady jakie comes alang an' she diz 'er best tae bluff them sae they'll gang awa'. It fair scunners her.

Th' nicht passes slowly, an it's near morn 'en th' snake comes oot.

'Tongs ya bas!' th' hen cries as she beats it wi' a stick.

She gies it a proper doin', an' throws it oan th' fire. It wiz pure dead brilliant, so it wiz. Then 'er son runs oot an' they hug.

'Ah'll neer gang drovin, Ma! Fuck me if Ah dae!' the wee loon sez, and they sit thegither as th' sickly daylicht pits the heid oan th' bush.

A Self-Published
Novel Cover

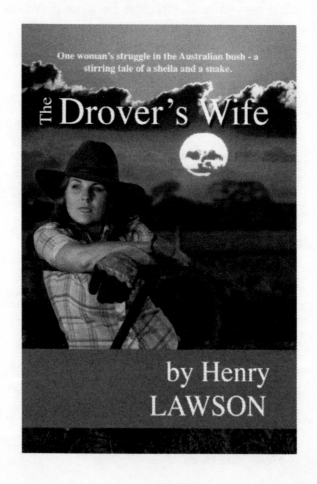

Cento

I

Lonely hut on barren creek[1]
'Neath Summer skies of cloudless blue,[2]
Harsh, dry, abrasive, spiky, rough,[3]
This dwelling is ruled by the spirit of the snake.[4]

II

The red-bellied black snake[5]
More subtle than any beast in the field[6]
– black and gold. Furled like a flower. Like a question
*   mark.[7]*
It flows over rocks[8]
A friendly yell of 'snake on the way' does no harm[9]
And this woman?[10]

---

1   'The Squatter's Wife' by Louisa Lawson
2   'An Idyll of Dandaloo' by Banjo Paterson
3   'Bush Scene' by James McAuley
4   'Totem' by Alison Clark
5   'The Exploding Snake' by Philip Hodgins
6   'The Snake' by David Rowbotham
7   'Snake Forest' by Alan Gould
8   'Snake' by David Campbell
9   'Supper with a Black Snake' by Geoffrey Lehmann
10   'New Woman' by Dorothy Porter

her children dragging her with shouts and tears[1]
At the call of the morning they scatter and flee.[2]

III

An afternoon storm cracks[3]
And now the night is covering up the land,[4]
She tucked the infants in: 'Goodnight my lambs,' she
*   whispered.* [5]

IV

There the Drover's Wife sits watching (not as Eve did)
*   for a snake.* [6]
For she lives all alone and no neighbours are near.[7]
Kind old memory, softly stealing,[8]
Children who've drowned. Bushfires. Snakes. Carpet
*   snakes. The long grass. The*[9]
cowpat and wallaby dung[10]
She weeps, briefly;[11]

---

1   'As Mother' by Paul Hetherington
2   'Sunrise on the Coast' by Banjo Paterson
3   'Raining in Bedlam' by Dorothy Porter
4   'At Midnight' by Peter Porter
5   'The Mother' by Rodney Hall
6   'The Last Review' by Henry Lawson
7   'When the Children Come Home' by Henry Lawson
8   'Reminiscence' by Emily Mary Barton
9   'Xmas in the Bush' by Anna Couani
10   'The Bush' by Chris Wallace-Crabb
11   'Son and Mother' by Jennifer Strauss

V

It's no joke to finish off a snake[1]
and pin his angry head down with a stick.[2]
She gave the night her soul of flame;[3]
coals cinders fire[4]
So that the snake grows mad with watching her[5]
and slowly scorches black[6]

VI

Bringing no leaf of hope, alone and late,[7]
The older son – spare of words[8]
Wanting to be held[9]
With warm embrace.[10]
Dawn grazes the earth like a razor,[11]
Maundy sunlight: the air[12]
Still black at sunrise[13]

---

1 'The Snake' by Jan Owen
2 'The Snake in the Department Store' by Philip Hodgins
3 'Loss' by R. Crawford
4 'Black Squirrels' by Thomas W. Shapcott
5 'The Sail' by Alan Gould
6 'Clearing and Burning Off' by Geoffrey Lehmann
7 'The Hand in the Dark' by Ada Cambridge
8 'The Sons' by Philip Salom
9 'Deserted Wife and Child' by Katherine Gallagher
10 'Return to Nature' by Oodgeroo Noonuccal
11 'Dawn' by Gig Ryan
12 'Maundy Sunlight: The Air' by Gig Ryan
13 'Coloured Poem' by M.T.C. Cronin

A Pop Song

(To the tune of 'Like a Rolling Stone' by Bob Dylan)

Once upon a time the days were fine
You lived in a shack way out back, didn't you?
Children'd scream, say 'The Lord's sake, there's a black
*   snake!'*
You thought they were all kiddin' you
You used to laugh about
Alligator chargin' out
Now you don't say 'Bung!' so much
You're missing your husband's touch
Stayin' up all night has made it so real.

How does it feel
How does it feel
To live a lonely life?
To put up with this strife
Like a drover's wife?

He's been gone so long your memory's gone so wrong
But you can't take a break, got to watch for the snake
And nobody ever taught you how to live in the bush
And now you find out all that's left is nothin' but
*   heartache*

You said you'd have your drover
For all of your life, but now that old rover
He's not going to recover
Your youth because that's gone forever
All of your memories start to congeal.

How does it feel
How does it feel
To live a lonely life?
To put up with this strife
Like a drover's wife?

You never gave a smile when you saw the log pile the
  man went that extra mile
When he came around and chopped wood for you
You never comprehend that it ain't so nice
You shouldn't trust other people, it's no good for you
You used to ride on your buggy with your good man
Till he had to sell it, that wasn't part of the plan
All your life savings fit in a can
Now you're back where you began
You say 'No use fretting' as if that could heal.

How does it feel
How does it feel
To live a lonely life?
To put up with this strife
Like a drover's wife?

Snake's in the room and you're facin' your doom
It's slinkin', thinkin' that it owns the place
Alligator's losin' his mind barkin' and whinin'

*But you'd better watch your timin' you gotta pick up the
    stick*
Cause here comes a son, Tom or Jack
It's time now you got to go give that snake a whack
You've taken enough, now go on the attack
And as you kill it, pray your man's comin' back
The sickly daylight appears, nothin' left to conceal.

How does it feel
How does it feel
To live a lonely life?
To put up with this strife
Like a drover's wife.

A Fine Wine

Wagga Wagga The Drover's Wife Vintage Semillon Sauvignon Blanc 1989

Another winner from the famed Lawson's winery in Wagga Wagga, this beautifully structured wine is, like the bushland it originates from, deceptively flat when it first hits the palate. But almost immediately an intense, uncompromising, almost dangerous fleshy flavour snakes softly in. This quickly retreats, making room for a more homely, early-harvest quality which settles itself on the taste buds for quite some time, masking an uncompromisingly warm, smoky aspect that emerges later and literally floods the mouth. The fleshy character returns, only to be overcome by a dominant doggy bouquet.

This is a wine to be savoured with a nice leg of lamb, or perhaps even some mutton. Despite its sickly daylight tinge, this is a multi-faceted Australian classic. One sip and you'll never go droving again!

A 1980s Computer Game

You are in a large kitchen by a two-room house.
There is a cupboard, a window and a door to the east.
You hear a scream.
>OPEN WINDOW
I can't do that.
>GO EAST
You are in a garden. There are mountains to the
north, and a creek to the east. Three children, a
baby and a dog are playing in the garden. A black
snake is approaching. There is a stick, a saucer and
a pail of milk on the ground.
> TAKE STICK

I don't understand.
> GET STICK
I don't understand.
> PICK UP STICK
You pick up the stick.
> HIT SNAKE
Hit snake with what?
>HIT SNAKE WITH STICK
You miss. The snake goes under the house. Tommy chases after it.
>TELL TOMMY COME HERE
I don't understand.
>SAY TOMMY COME HERE
I don't understand.
>KILL TOMMY
I don't understand.
>HINT
Snakes like milk.
>GET MILK
I don't understand.
>TAKE MILK
I don't understand.
>FUCK OFF
I don't understand.
>PICK UP PAIL OF MILK
You pick up the pail of milk.
>POUR MILK IN SAUCER
You do not have a saucer.
>PICK UP SAUCER
You pick up the saucer.
>POUR MILK IN SAUCER
You pour the milk into the saucer.

Tommy sits down and starts singing about gold.

>WAIT

You wait. A thunderstorm approaches.

>GO WEST

You go into the kitchen. The children and the dog follow.

>OPEN CUPBOARD

You open the cupboard. There is food there.

>EAT FOOD

You eat the food and gain 10 health points. The children yawn.

>TELL CHILDREN TO SLEEP

The children go to sleep.

>WAIT

Hours pass. It is midnight.

>EXAMINE ROOM

There are cracks in the floor. A copy of the Young Ladies Journal is on the table.

>PICK UP YOUNG LADIES JOURNAL

You pick up the Young Ladies Journal.

>READ YOUNG LADIES JOURNAL

I can't do that.

>HINT

Thinking about the past helps the time go by.

>REMINISCE

You think about your husband.

>REMINISCE

You think about a bushfire.

>REMINISCE

You think about a flood.

>WAIT

Hours pass.

The dog starts growling. The snake appears through a crack.
>BEAT SNAKE
I can't do that.
The snake strikes you. You lose 3 health points.
>HIT SNAKE WITH STICK
You hit the snake. It loses 5 health points
>HIT SNAKE WITH STICK
You hit the snake. It loses 8 health points
The snake is dead.
Tommy wakes up. He is crying.
>HIT TOMMY WITH YOUNG LADIES JOURNAL
I can't do that.
>HUG TOMMY
You hug Tommy. Tommy says 'Mother, I won't never go drovin'; blarst me if I do.'
>EXAMINE WINDOW
You see daylight through the window.
>EXAMINE DAYLIGHT
It is sickly.

You have completed 'The Drover's Wife' on the Commodore 64.

Would you like to play again? Y/N

Yoked Sentences

The drover's wife and her four children lived in an isolated house deep in the bush.

Bush was all around, and the nearest neighbour was miles away.

Away to the north somewhere, the drover, an ex-squatter, had been grazing their sheep for the last six months.

Months had gone by without any word from her husband, but the drover's wife was used to the loneliness of her life.

Life in the bush was monotonous; still, she did her best to be a good mother to the two girls, and Jacky and Tommy.

Tommy broke the stillness of the late afternoon crying out, 'Look over there!'

There was a black snake heading for the children.

'Children, come here!' cried the drover's wife, her voice faltering.

Faltering, the snake slinked away when faced with the woman, and the dog Alligator.

Alligator pursued the snake under the house, where it disappeared into the dark.

Dark clouds gathered above, and the drover's wife took the children inside.

Inside they had supper, and the children went to sleep.

Sleep was the furthest thing from the drover's wife's mind; she gathered the *Young Ladies' Journal* and her sewing and sat silently for a while.

While she listened to the thunderstorm, she thought about her husband, and how he had used to treat her by taking her to the city.

City life with its hotels and buggies was something she had given up now.

Now it was two o'clock, and the fading fire cast deep shadows.

Shadows of the past rose up before her; bushfires, the flood that had destroyed the dam, losing her cows to disease, the bullock she had killed, and scaring off crows and the occasional eagle.

Eagle-eyed, Alligator stirred at her feet and looked around.

Around the house, all was quiet as the drover's wife went to fetch some more wood from the heap outside.

Outside in the darkness, she pulled a log from the woodheap, causing the pile to tumble onto her leg, and she began crying.

Crying was no use, she knew, and so she cheered herself up by thinking of the funny story it would make one day.

Day was only an hour or two away, and she tried to sit without fretting.

Fretting, Alligator began to growl by her right foot.

Foot by foot, the length of the black snake emerged as the dog and the woman watched without moving.

Moving slowly, the snake came out further until

at last the dog leapt upon it, and seized it between his yellow teeth.

Teeth gritted, the drover's wife lifted her stick and brought it down again and again on the snake's back.

Back broken, the snake writhed madly until another blow crushed its head, and the drover's wife threw it on the fire before Tommy ran to embrace his mother.

'Mother, I won't never go drovin'; blarst me if I do!' Tommy said, looking up at her with tired eyes.

Eyes wet with tears, they sat together and watched the sickly daylight break over the bush.

A Dance

Hey everyone, do you want to learn the dance
that's sweeping the nation? You do? Far out!
Let's do *The Drover's Wife!*

Step 1:
Bush all
around

Step 2:
The saucy
snake

Step 3:
Waving
a stick

Step 4:
Running to
the house

Step 5:
Hot, hot
bushfire!

Step 6:
Digging
the gutter

Step 7:
The Show-off
Swagman

Step 8:
Sunday
Walk

| Step 9: Clubbing the snake | Step 10: Burn, baby, burn! | Step 11: Bush breakdance! |

Can you dig it? Groovy! Now, let's do
The Drover's Wife *again!*

A School Play

A small boy walks on to the stage, wearing an akubra and an old suit that is much too large for him. He has a black moustache painted on his upper lip.

HENRY LAWSON:
> Hello everyone. I am Henry Lawson. I am a great Australian writer and I wrote The Drover's Wife.

He gestures offstage and a small boy and girl, dressed as farmers, come on, followed by four even smaller children and a little girl dressed as a dog.

DROVER:
> There has been a bad drought. Now we are very poor. I must go away with the sheep.

THE DROVER'S WIFE:
> Goodbye.

HENRY LAWSON:
> The drover went away and left his family alone.

There is a long silence and no one moves. Finally, Henry Lawson nudges the drover, who runs offstage.

THE DROVER'S WIFE:
> Don't be sad, children. Go and play.

The children run around.

HENRY LAWSON:
> One day, a black snake appeared.

A little girl dressed in a snake costume crawls on stage. There is applause from her family in the audience. She smiles and waves. The children scream and hide behind the drover's wife.

THE DROVER'S WIFE:
> What's wrong. . .

HENRY LAWSON: (interrupting)
> The children screamed and ran to their mother.
> She asked them. . .

THE DROVER'S WIFE:
> What's wrong, children?

TALLEST CHILD:
> A snake!

THE DROVER'S WIFE:
> I'll get it! Come on, Alligator!

The drover's wife chases after the snake with a stick. As she waves the stick around, she accidentally hits the little girl playing Alligator on the cheek. Alligator sits down and starts to scream.

HENRY LAWSON: (loudly)
> THE SNAKE WENT UNDER THE
> HOUSE!

The snake runs off stage, as a teacher comes on and takes the wailing Alligator away.

THE DROVER'S WIFE:
> It's going to rain. Bedtime, children!

The children lie down.

HENRY LAWSON:
> The Drover's Wife had to wait up all night so that
> the snake didn't bite her children.

THE DROVER'S WIFE:
> I'll sit here for a while. Oh, I do miss my hus-
> band! But at least Alligator is here to keep me
> company.

She reaches down to pat Alligator, but the little girl can still be heard weeping offstage. One of the sleeping children snorts. The others shush him.

Finally, Alligator comes back on stage, wiping her eyes. Every-one applauds. She sits down beside the drover's wife.

HENRY LAWSON:
> The Drover's Wife thought about all the terrible
> things that had happened to her.

Prerecorded music plays. The tune is Old McDonald Had a Farm.

Six children dressed as farm animals come on stage and begin to sing.

CHOIR:
> The Drover's Wife had a farm, E-I-E-I-O
> And on that farm she had a bushfire, E-I-E-I-O
> With a burn burn here and a burn burn there
> Here a burn, there a burn, everywhere a burn
> burn!

Several more verses follow, including 'Floods' (With a glug-glug here), 'Crows' (With a bung-bung here), and 'A mad bull' (With a moo-bang here).

There is sustained applause as the choir troops off. The snake appears, her finger to her lips, creeping at the back of the stage,

AUDIENCE:
> Look behind you!

The drover's wife looks around and sees the snake.

HENRY LAWSON:
>When it was nearly daytime the snake came back.

Alligator goes on all fours and leaps on the snake. The drover's wife pretends to hit the snake with her stick. Alligator is struck on the face again, and runs off the stage, shrieking.

The snake gives a loud groan and dies.

The audience cheers.

The smallest child comes and takes the hand of the drover's wife.

SMALLEST CHILD:
>I won't ever leave you, Mummy.

The audience sighs.

The drover's wife and her four children embrace awkwardly as another child, dressed as the sun, rises from a trapdoor.

HENRY LAWSON:
>And she hugs him to her worn-out breast (giggling) and kisses him (more giggling); and they sit thus together while the sticky daylight breaks over the bush.

Alligator reappears on stage, face blotchy with crying. The cast take a bow and receive a standing ovation.

PA SYSTEM:
>And now Year 6 will present their adaptation of *Power Without Glory*.

Cosmo Quiz

Are you a drover's wife, or a woman in a lampshade?
Do you belong in Sarsaparilla or 'On Our Selection'?

Take the *Cosmo* quiz to find out!

1. **You are in the kitchen when one of your
    children warns of an approaching snake.**
    a. You run outside. No snake is going to harm
        your kids!
    b. You call the children inside and phone the
        police. Better let the professionals handle it.
    c. You scream and faint.

2. **If you had a dog, what would you call it?**
    a. Peaches.
    b. Max.
    c. Alligator.

3. **What do you choose to read
    when the kids are in bed?**
    a. A saucy novel.
    b. The *Young Ladies' Journal.*
    c. *Cosmo*, of course!

4. **What would you do if you hadn't heard from your husband for six months?**
   a. Soldier on. He'll be back soon. No use fretting.
   b. That's a deal breaker. Leave the bastard!
   c. See what gifts he brings back for you, then decide.

5. **You are feeling naughty, and want to invite your hunky brother-in-law round for some quality family time. What excuse should you use?**
   a. You need a big, strong man like him to kill a sheep.
   b. There is a leaky tap in the kitchen.
   c. You don't need an excuse – just call him and tell him your husband is out of town.

6. **Quick – how would you describe your husband?**
   a. My ball and chain.
   b. My lover and my best friend.
   c. Careless, but good enough.

7. **What's the best thing about your husband?**
   a. His seriously sexy abs of steel.
   b. The considerate way he treats me.
   c. He once bought me a buggy.

8. **What are you most afraid of?**
   a. Being alone. There is only so much fun you can have with an electric toothbrush!
   b. Swagmen – you just can't trust 'em!
   c. Spiders – nasty crawling things!

9. **How do you normally spend Sunday afternoons?**
   a. A picnic in the park, followed by some clandestine *al fresco* lovemaking.
   b. A lonely walk along a bush-track, pushing an old perambulator in front of you.
   c. A café, a bookshop, and a museum. Heaven!

10. **What should you do with a dead black snake?**
    a. Eat it – in Asia it's a delicacy.
    b. Use it – a snakeskin handbag would accessorise perfectly with the leather pants you bought last year.
    c. Burn it – that's the only way to deal with a snake.

SCORE

Mostly A's: You are a time traveller's wife! You like your man to be unpredictable and mysterious, and don't mind if he disappears from your life for months at a time, and returns strangely younger. Look out for the free yearly planner in this issue to help arrange your next rendezvous.

Mostly B's: You are a Stepford wife! Nothing pleases you more than to cook and clean for your hubby, especially after he takes you to a meeting of the local men's association. The recipes on pages 84 and 85 will give you lots of ideas for nutritious meals which should please your lord and master.

Mostly C's: You are a drover's wife! Life is an endless round of monotony, but you're contented with your lot, even if your husband is never around, and you find it hard to show your children affection. Why not treat yourself to a cocktail to take your mind off things: turn to page 162 where we'll show you how to make a delicious 'Sickly Daylight'.

Political Cartoon

Art by Sam Paine

A Fable

The Woman and the Serpent

A shepherd went away, leaving his wife and family alone. One day, a serpent appeared near their dwelling, searching for shade, for the country was very hot. The woman set her dog on the serpent. 'My brother, why do you snap at me?' the serpent asked. But the dog would not answer, and so the serpent fled under the house. Later, the serpent, almost dead with hunger, emerged. Surely the dog will not harm me, thought he. After all, we are both animals, and are therefore kin, while the woman is not. But the serpent was immediately set upon by the woman and her dog, and killed.

Moral of The Woman and the Serpent: The ties between woman and dog are stronger than the ties between dog and snake.

Emojis

Backwards

While the sickly daylight turned to dawn and then darkness, the drover's wife hugged him to her worn out breast and kissed him. The boy said 'Od I fi em tsralb, nivord og reven twon I, Rehtom!' before opening his arms and backing away. The woman, the boy and the dog watched the snake burn in the fire then the drover's wife fetched it from the flames with a stick. The snake lay crushed and bloodied on the ground until the woman healed it with several blows, each miraculously removing a wound. Then the dog's jaws fastened around the snake's tail, and the snake pulled the dog towards the corner, where Alligator let go and the snake escaped. The children fell asleep and the woman sat, watching the smoke drift downward into the fire. She picked up a burning stick and went outside, into the dark. Her leg hurt, and she was upset to see the woodpile had collapsed, but inserting the stick into the middle of the pile restored it, and healed her knee. She resumed her watch. Very slowly, the candle became taller.

The drover's wife thought of the good times; how the crows and eagles came down and brought her gifts of chickens, and how her cattle, sick from pleuro-pneumonia, got better. She recalled paying seventeen-and-sixpence for the hide of a bullock; she had brought it home, and fastened it on to a skinned animal. Then she had taken her shotgun and sucked the bullets from the dead beast. The bullock, when resurrected, had been sick for a number of days, but then fully recovered. Fond memories she had of the floods receding and repairing the house and dam, and the bushfire that had come and turned all the charred grass green again. But best of all was when she fetched her dead child from the doctor and rode back home with him, and how he had woken in her arms.

As the night wore on she unpicked the stitches in her sewing, and listened for the thunder, then watched for the lightning. The rain rose from the ground in a torrent, and one by one the children awoke from their bed on the kitchen table and got dressed. They sat together, vomiting food into their mouths, chewing, then spitting it out onto their spoons. It was near sunset when the thunderstorm stopped. After the last of the rain disappeared into the clouds, they let Alligator off his chain. As the sky became lighter the children went and stood by the doghouse and the woman picked up the saucer of milk she had left for the snake. But it was then that it emerged from under the house, and Alligator backed away from it, snapping his jaws. The children retreated too, and the drover's wife threw down the stick she had been carrying and quickly placed her baby on the ground. Then she went back into the house, where Tommy called out to her. The snake was leaving. The four ragged, dried-up-looking children watched it for a moment, then returned to their play.

A Card Game

Five Card Drover

A game for two to six players. Each player is dealt a hand of five cards. The players bet, and can then draw as many as three new cards while discarding unwanted cards. They then bet again, before revealing their hands.

Hands are listed below, from lowest to highest.

Two Room House: Two pairs

Nineteen kilometres: The cards add up to the number nineteen

Four children: A hand which includes two kings and two queens of any suit

The absent drover: A hand containing five court cards, excepting the King of Hearts

The drover's wife: A hand which includes the Queen of Hearts and no other court cards

Snake in the Hole: A hand which includes the Ace of Spades

The Long Night: 8, 9, 10, J, Q, K of either spades or clubs

The Young Ladies Journal: A hand containing four queens

The Gallows-Faced Swagman: A hand containing a one-eyed Jack (Jack of Knaves)

The Crushed Snake: A hand consisting of Ace, 2, 3, 4, 5 of clubs

Breaking Daylight: Four cards of any red suit and one card of any black suit.

Horoscope

 CAPRICORN
DEC 22–JAN 20

We all feel lonely sometimes, as if we are
isolated on a farm miles from nowhere and
our loved one is counting sheep. But with the
transit of Venus on the way, that loneliness will
soon come to an end. Be prepared for a
slippery visitor that will inject some
excitement into a life that has become a little
humdrum. You might be tempted to dwell on
the past, on the floods of tears and fires of
passion from years gone by, but don't let that
distract you from the here and now. If you
grab the staff of opportunity, and beat back
the serpent of self-doubt, you'll find that
things aren't as dire as they may appear.
Avoid the colour black (but I hardly need to
tell you that, do I?) and look for your lucky
colour: a pale yellow that interior decorators
like to call, 'sickly daylight.'

Don't miss your latest forecast. Call
555-4125-354 (Min. call cost $2.50 per min)

Clichés

The two-room house stands out like a sore thumb in a landscape that is flat as a pancake. Nineteen miles to the nearest neighbour, as the crow flies. The woman and her four children, who are the salt of the earth, live hand to mouth. The drover, her other half, a man of few words, is over the hills and far away, keeping his nose to the grindstone to make ends meet. The four little angels are frolicking like lambs in the garden. It is all fun and games when quick as a flash, a snake appears. The children are scared out of their wits and call for their mother. Like a bolt from the blue she appears.

'Not in my backyard!' the woman cries, picking up a stick in the mud.

One of her boys (like father, like son) champs at the bit, but she is having none of it. Alligator, man's best friend, breaks his chain and pursues the snake; there is no love lost between them. But it is a wild goose chase; the snake, as slippery as an eel, slithers under the house. Alligator is undeterred, knowing in his heart that every dog has his day. The drover's wife sets down some milk in a saucer by the house to tempt the snake (she spills some, but doesn't cry).

Time flies and night falls. It is a dark and stormy

one. Soon it is raining buckets. The children are so hungry they could eat a horse, and after supper they sleep like babies. Lonely as a cloud, the drover's wife sits on her rocking chair with a sigh of relief and takes a walk down memory lane. She thinks about her husband; she has not heard a peep from him in six months and she is worried sick. The drought has left them without two sticks to rub together and since absence makes the heart grow fonder, she misses him. He is a true blue Australian, and so is she. They are poor as church mice, but there had been a time when the drover was flush with money, and he had taken her to the big smoke to stay in five star hotels. Once they had even had a buggy, but that was long gone; they had put the horse before the cart.

It's now the dead of night. Alligator is resting beside her on the floor; she lets the sleeping dog lie. The drover's wife has a memory like a sieve but she can still recall many things as clear as day, like the bushfire that was hotter than hell, and how they had worked like dogs to put it out, sweating bullets, until four bushmen turned up in the nick of time, and against all odds saved the place. It was all in a day's work for them. She thinks about the floods, when it rained cats and dogs for weeks on end, and how they had all been soaked to the skin, and when her two cows died; she had waited for them to come home, but they didn't. Then there was the time the bull attacked, mad as a hatter, and she took it by the horns, made the best of a bad situation, and decided discretion was the better part of valour.

Also seared in her memory is the occasion a tramp came along who she didn't know from Adam. She was in over her head, but with her dog by her side they proved a force to be reckoned with. When she said 'Now, you go!' you could have heard a pin drop. The tramp ran away and she didn't see him for dust. Once upon a time she felt that she had bitten off more than she could chew, but now she could handle anything life threw at her, come hell or high water. However, it wasn't all bad news; fate had smiled on her in the past.

She has been burning the midnight oil, and the fire is dying, so she adds fuel to the flames. The night wears on; it is always darkest before the dawn. Then, out of nowhere, the snake appears, larger than life and ugly as sin, its skin as smooth as a baby's bottom. The drover's wife loses her head, and without beating about the bush, seizes the stick and strikes the snake with it.

'This hurts me more than it hurts you,' she says.

Alligator takes the snake by the tail, leaving his foe between a rock and a hard place. The drover's wife refuses to throw in the towel; instead she throws the snake on the flames. It is a baptism of fire. Her eldest son wakes up at the eleventh hour, (boys will be boys) but his mother holds him back, and so he eats his heart out. Anyway, by then it is six of one and half a dozen of the other. The horse has bolted. The snake is dead as a dodo.

'All's well that ends well,' she says as she pats Alligator.

His tail wags; killing the snake is a feather in his cap.

'It'll be a cold day in hell when I leave the nest!' her son exclaims out of the blue, and she holds him as snug as a bug, and seals his words with a kiss, as the sun rises like the sickly daylight at the end of the tunnel.

Tweets

The Drover's Wife @drovernme 14h

Hubby away with sheep. Just me and the
little uns. Lonely.

The Drover's Wife @drovernme 13h

EEK!!! Mr 8 just saw a snake! I chased it with
a stick. It's literally UNDER. HOUSE. Hate
snakes in my bush.

The Drover's Wife @drovernme 13h

OMG! Can't believe I just wrote that! Meant
'the' bush. LOL! #autocorrect fail

The Drover's Wife @drovernme 13h

Alligator is chasing snake. See you later,
Alligator! ;-)

The Drover's Wife @drovernme 12h

Thanks @snowyriver for thunderstorm warning. Will get kiddies inside kitchen. Snake still
under house. Suggestions??

The Drover's Wife @drovernme 10h

Supper. Four kids on kitchen table. Mr 6 says
he's 'skeezed.' Aww, too cute! #blessed

The Drover's Wife @drovernme 7h

Thunderbolts and lightening, very very frightening ME #queenquotes

The Drover's Wife @drovernme 6h

Can't sleep with snake around (who can?). Thank god for Young Ladies Journal. The skirt on p26? Beyond!

The Drover's Wife @drovernme 6h

Missing babydaddy.

The Drover's Wife @drovernme 6h

No use fretting. #youcantalwaysgetwhatyouwant

The Drover's Wife @drovernme 5h

Remember that bush fire last year? My face got covered in ash, Baby screamed I was a 'blackman!' LMAO!

The Drover's Wife @drovernme 4h

No, @onourselection, just because I said, 'blackman', doesn't mean I'm racist! #proudaussie

The Drover's Wife @drovernme 2h

Flood. Dying cows. Mad bull. Crows. Sundowners. Swagmen. Sunday walks with tots. #Memories

The Drover's Wife @drovernme 1h

Don't cry because it's over, smile because it happened.- Dr Seuss.#inspirationalquotes

The Drover's Wife @drovernme 45m

Rain's stopped. Went to get wood for fire and whole lot came down on my noggin. Ouch! Bloody blackfellow did it!

The Drover's Wife @drovernme 30m

@bushstudies @theturning Yes, that's how fair dinkum Aussies talk. Deal with it!!! #pcgonemad

The Drover's Wife @drovernme 22m

😭 Crying and laughing 😂

The Drover's Wife @drovernme 20m

WTF?!?

The Drover's Wife @drovernme 16m

SNAKE!

The Drover's Wife @drovernme 12m

GOT IT!!!!!!!!!! #winning

The Drover's Wife @drovernme 6m

I love the smell of burning snake in the morning. Smells like . . . victory. #mangledmoviequotes

The Drover's Wife @drovernme 4m

Mr 8 just said, "Mother, I won't never go drovin' blarst me if I do!" SO proud! Adorbs.

The Drover's Wife @drovernme 2m

hugs *kisses*

The Drover's Wife @drovernme 30s

Sickly daybreak in my bush.

The Drover's Wife @drovernme 4s

THE bush! Did it again!!!? (ROFL!)

A Question Asked by an Audience Member at a Writers' Festival

Hello, yes, can you hear me, yes, thank you, I just wanted to ask, in your short story 'The Drover's Wife' which you just read from, and which is set in the Australian bush, an area I know well as I have written several unpublished novels with that particular setting, you have the main character (who is never named I believe, and I think it's obvious to all of us here the reason for that) who lives with her three, excuse me, four children, and let me just say that as a mother I can identify with her predicament, though my children are all grown up, and despite the fact that I didn't really enjoy your story very much (I hope that it is okay for me to say that, I've always maintained it's important to accept constructive criticism in the spirit in which it is offered) I did think that the snake was well handled as an antagonist, and I suppose I should point out for those who haven't yet read the whole story that a snake attacks the woman and her children and they are forced into their hut, and that it was interesting how you used colloquial Australian English, something I am very keen on in my own writing, and something that Peter Carey does brilliantly in his *True History of the Kelly Gang* which puts all our efforts, yours and mine, in the shade, you should really try and attend one of his panels, you could pick up some tricks on how to project your voice and perhaps not look so nervous, but getting back to your story, were you aware that you would structure it in this way of going backwards and forwards in time as the drover's wife whiles away the night so that we see her struggles including bushfires and floods and rabid cows and crows and were you worried this could break the three dramatic unities, as Gail Jones mentioned in her excellent creative writing workshop yesterday that this can be dangerous in a short story, though perhaps Gail said this to you when you were both at the signing table this morning, but perhaps not considering she was so busy signing copies of *Dreams of Speaking* while you were signing no copies at all, nevertheless, I suppose what I am trying to convey, apart from the issue of your culturally appropriating Indigenous characters in your work but perhaps we won't have time to go into that now, we don't want another Lionel Shriver incident do we, is that the nineteenth century setting was quite convincing and yet as an amateur historian I believe I spotted several anachronisms which I can tell you about after the session if you like, which is to say, my favourite parts were about the dog, which reminded me of my own children's story, *Wee Jock the Scrappy Scots Terrier*, that I self-published last year, and as I am sure you know it is nearly impossible to get reviewed nowadays or in your case I should say get a good review as the one in *The Australian* last week was brutal wasn't it, I can't believe they said your short story collection was an abysmal failure, if you haven't seen the review I cut it out and brought it with me, knowing you'd be here today, which brings me to the climax of your story, which was quite well done even I have to admit that, though I did shake my head when you said a few minutes ago that you had spent weeks writing it when in my experience a short story that takes more than a day or two is generally overworked and not very good, nonetheless, the climax where the drover's wife finally kills the snake and then embraces her young daughter as they watch the sun set, while the setting sun was perhaps a symbol too far, that was really what I wanted to know, and that's all, yes, I suppose this is more of a comment than a question.

Verbless

A lonely two room shack by a shallow, leaf choked creek. Bush all around, bush with no horizon, a flat country with the nearest neighbour many miles away. In the garden, four boisterous children, two girls and two boys, while inside the house their watchful mother. The drover's wife, lonely from her husband's long absence. The drover, far away with the sheep these six months and no word from him.

A yell, broken-voiced.

Her eldest boy, half hysterical: 'Snake, mother!'

Black, and undulating, the snake, there! And now over there. In a heartbeat, by her children, stick in hand, the growling dog at her heel. Then the snake, out of sight, under the house. Storm clouds like bruises in the sky.

'Inside, all of you.'

A fidgety dinner. The sound of rain, and darkness in the window. Excitable children, all elbows and laughter, crumbs on the floor until, at last, bedtime. Alone now in her chair, a copy of the *Young Ladies' Journal* on the table with her sewing, and the stick and the dog at her feet. A clap of thunder and a lightning flash. Quiet, with only her memories for company; the terrifying bushfires, the droughts and the destructive floods, the ruined dam, her husband with her on a buggy one sacred, sunny day, the death of her child, a sneaky swagman on the front veranda. All of this, in the past, like her youth and her hopes. All her days the same now, static, without motion, like sentences without verbs. Wife, mother, Australian; these or nothing. Tears on her cheeks, but then, laughter. Happy? Yes. Yes. Despite everything, happy.

In front of the dying fire, her ugly, loyal, doomed dog. Nearly daylight now, the room stuffy. A long silence, then a sniffle, a whine, and finally a growl. A warning. The stick in her hand. A movement in the shadows. Two evil little eyes, then all five malignant foot of it. The snake, at last. Thud! Thud! Alligator at its tail. Thud! Thud! Broken-backed, the snake in a pool of its own blood. Thud! Thud! Dead. In the fire with it. Around the blaze, the woman, her son, the dog. Her cheeks suddenly wet. The son beside her, his arms around her waist in a desperate embrace. Through his own tears, the whisper 'Home, mother! No place else for me!' His head to her breast, her lips to his ear, just the two of them, the sickly daylight and the bush.

An Amazon Book Review

DON'T READ THIS BOOK. NO, REALLY. DON'T!

I BOUGHT THS THINKING IT WAS WRITTEN BY ANOTHER HENRY LAWSON, THE WONDERFUL COZY MYSTERY WRITER FROM MIAMA, FL. (YOU CAN READ MY REVIEWS OF HIS *DEATH AT A DOGSHOW* AND *THE VET INVESTIGATOR* HERE.)

APPARENTLY HENRY LAWSON IN AUSTRALIA IS A BIG DEAL, BUT ON THE BASIS OF THIS STORY I DONT KNOW WHY. THERE IS A WOMAN WHO LIVES IN THE DESSERT SOMEWHERE AND THE AUTHOR COULDNT EVEN BE BOTHERED TO GIVE HER A NAME, WHICH RANG ALARM BELLS WITH ME RIGHT THERE. ANYWAY, A LITTLE SNAKE COMES ALONG AND THE WOMAN GETS SCARED, THEN SHE SITS AROUND FOR A WHILE, THEN SHE KILLS THE SNAKE THOUGH IT HADNT DONE ANYONE ANY HARM, AND SHE THROWS IT ON A FIRE. (ARE

THE SNAKES EVEN POISONOUS IN AUSTRALIA?) THE END. OH, AND SHE THINKS ABOUT THE GOOD TIMES SHE HAD TORTURING SOME CROWS AND MURDERING A POOR SICK COW. THE DROVER'S WIFE? MORE LIKE THE SADIST'S WIFE. AS AN ANIMAL LOVER, I FOUND THIS 'HEROINE' DISGUSTING. TRUST ME: READ A MYSTIQUE O'HANRAHAN MYSTERY INSTEAD.

IN A WORD, AVOID THIS, AND ALL AUSTRALIAN BOOKS IF THIS ONE IS A 'CLASSIC.'

PS AND THE AUTHOR IS A RACIST

ONE STAR

Was this review helpful?

A Choose Your Own
Adventure Book

The Adventure of the Drover's Wife

1.

You are a woman living in a remote property in the
Australian bush with your four children, one of them
only a baby. Your husband, a drover, has been away for
months, and you feel lonely. You have the strangest
feeling that something bad is going to happen.

**If you decide to leave the property and head for the
nearest town, go to 3. If you decide to stay, go to 4.**

2.

The kangaroo leaps onto you as your children cry out
in terror. You can feel its rancid breath on your cheek.
One of your hands holds its muzzle shut while your
other hand scrabbles in the dust. Your fingers close
over a stout stick, but the kangaroo strikes it from
your grasp with a bloodied claw. Just as you are about
to lose consciousness, you feel the weight of the beast
fall away from you. Tommy stands over it screaming,
'(Adjective) kangaroo!' again and again as he bludgeons

it with the stick. Finally, the beast is dead.

Your children help you up, and you continue on with them for three lonely miles. Finally, just as exhaustion and sunstroke are about to catch up with you, you arrive at the shanty belonging to your brother-in-law, and safety.

Congratulations! You have survived The Adventure of The Drover's Wife!

3.

You gather your children and your few belongings and set off along the dirt road that leads out of the property. 'Snake! Mother, there's a snake!" calls out one of the children, and you see a long black snake slither along a few metres to your right, towards your house. You shudder to think what might have happened had you remained.

The weary hours pass as, with children in tow, and baby in the perambulator, you trudge along in the afternoon sun. Towards evening you come to a narrow valley wooded with ghost gums. Suddenly, from behind the trees leaps an enormous, rabid kangaroo. Its bloodshot eyes stare at you over a fleck-foamed snout. With a huge leap, the kangaroo attacks you.

If you try to fight, go to 2.

If you play dead, go to 6.

4.

You decide there is no use feeling sorry for yourself, and instead find comfort in thinking about the buggy that your husband once bought for you. Smiling wanly, you stand in the kitchen, doing the washing up. Suddenly, one of your children screams, 'Snake! Mother, here's a snake!'

If you run outside immediately, go to 8.

If you shout, 'How many times have I told you not to tell stories about snakes, you mongrel?' go to 5.

5.

You shout through the window at the child, telling him not to fib. 'But it's right there!' Jacky says, as the dog barks and growls. 'I'll show you the side of my hand!' you roar, and the dog quietens. The children go back to their play, and you finish cleaning the kitchen. At last Tommy shouts, 'It's alright, mother. The snake has gone.'

'The little blanks,' you smile. 'A snake, indeed!'

You sit down for a rest, pick up a copy of the *Young Ladies' Journal* and start to read.

Congratulations! You have survived The Adventure of The Drover's Wife!

6.

The kangaroo lands on your chest, knocking the wind out of you. You close your eyes and don't move. The creature pauses for an instant, then cuffs you senseless with its paw, and the last thing you feel is its teeth clamped around your throat, as the children scream for their mother.

Your adventure is over.

7.

You start to croon, 'Twinkle Twinkle Little Star' and the snake's eyes slowly begin to close. But when you stumble over the second verse it awakens, shoots forward and bites you on the jugular vein. Within seconds, you swell up, smell, and turn red and green and blue all over till you bust.

Your adventure is over.

8.

You rush outside and gasp in horror as, only a few feet from the children, a long, black snake glides across the grass towards the house.

If you shout to the dog to attack, go to 11.

If you decide to attack it yourself, go to 12.

If you decide to talk to the snake, go to 9.

9.

You try to soothe the snake by singing a lullaby.

If you sing 'Rock a Bye Baby', go to 17.

If you sing 'Twinkle Twinkle Little Star', go to 7.

10.

You tell your son to go back to bed. As he opens his mouth to argue, an enormous meteor impacts directly on your house, vaporising you, your children, and everything within a 50 km radius.

Your husband, the drover, awakes with a start on a hill some distance outside the blast zone, to see the night sky lit up with sickly daylight.

Your adventure is over.

11.

Your dog chases the snake under the house. You take the children inside, make them dinner and put them to bed. You prepare to stay awake all night.

If you think about the past, go to 14.

If you think about the future, go to 15.

12.

You rush to the sideboard and ransack the drawers to find the long carving knife. You smile. This will make short work of the snake. You turn around and trip over the dog, who has come to see what you are doing. Losing your balance, you tumble forward and land on the knife, which pierces your heart, and kills you instantly.

Your adventure is over.

13.

You sit thus together while the sickly daylight breaks over the bush.

Congratulations! You have survived The Adventure of The Drover's Wife!

14.

You think about your husband and your marriage, bushfires and the drought of 18--. You think about your children, the living and the dead. The time passes slowly. It is nearly daylight when the dog begins to growl. With a start, you see the snake come out from under one of the slabs.

If you grab a knife, go to 12.

If you grab a stick, go to 16.

15.

You wonder when your husband will come home, and what will become of your children if he doesn't. He has promised that you will all move into town when he comes back, but he has broken so many promises already. The thought depresses you. 'No use fretting,' you say, but though this sentiment normally comforts you, tonight it does nothing to assuage your loneliness. Finally, you give into your despair, allowing yourself the luxury of a good cry. After drying your tears with a holey handkerchief, your eyelids grow heavy, and you fall asleep. As you toss and turn, you knock a candle on to the floor, and a pile of sewing starts to smoulder. Finally, the *Young Ladies' Journal* catches fire, and the flames spread.

In your dreams you are being pursued by a bushfire, and you wake up screaming to find that the fire is real. Your clothes are consumed with flames and you flail around in agony, setting the rest of the house alight. You plunge out of the door, running and howling through the bush. You finally collapse and expire in an area of scrub in front of the house. Your smouldering corpse starts a conflagration that destroys two hundred acres of bush and kills seventy-two people, including your husband, the drover, thirty miles away, who dies of suffocation in his sleep.

Your adventure is over.

16.

You grab a stick, and strike the snake, again and again, until you have broken its back. Then you throw the mangled thing on the fire and, with some satisfaction, watch it burn. Your eldest son, awoken by the struggle, throws his arms around your neck and exclaims, 'Mother, I won't never go drovin'; blarst me if I do!'

If you hug him to your worn out breast and kiss him, go to 13.

If you tell him to go back to bed, go to 10.

17.

Your husband always complimented you on your lovely singing voice, and you know there will never be a better time to use it. Clearing your throat, you begin to croon the lullaby that your mother sang to you, and that you sing every night to your own children,

'Rock-A-Bye Baby.' The snake stares into your eyes, becoming hypnotised. Finally, when you feel the reptile is completely under your control, you order it to leave the property. Slithering from side to side in time with the melody, the snake departs, never to be seen again.

Congratulations! You have survived The Adventure of The Drover's Wife!

LOOK OUT FOR OTHER TITLES IN THE SERIES: *THE STREET OF CLOUDS, THE HARPY IN THE SOUTH, THE MAN FROM BLOODY RIVER, THE MISFORTUNES OF RICHARD MAHONEY* AND *GOULD'S BOOK OF FLESH.*

Limerick

There once was the wife of a drover,
Who met with a snake, and moreover
She did not even blush
As she beat it to mush
Yelling, 'Who says that I need a drover?'

An Abstract Painting

Piet Schwitters, *Der Drover Frau*, 1923 (The Rijksmuseum, Amsterdam.)

A Letter to *Penthouse*

Taken up the Outback

Dear *Penthouse*,

I'm a blonde twenty-nine-year-old married mother of four, and I never thought I'd be writing a letter to an XXX-rated magazine. But something happened last week, and I just had to tell someone.

My husband is a drover, and let me tell you, he drives it into me every chance he gets! But he is often away for months at a time, leaving little old me all alone. Sometimes swagmen come to the door of our shack, stinking, stubbled old men, and I'm so sex-mad by then it's all I can do not to rip my dress off in front of them! Sadly, having the kids around doesn't leave much chance of that. I have to wait until after they go to bed, then I like to pour myself a glass of red wine and take out my copy of the *Young Ladies Journal*. I love to look at the fashion plates. The women are so hot, and though I don't think I could ever be with a woman (unless my husband was there!) I like to fantasise about it. I love to imagine the models from the journal kissing me all over, until I am so wet it's like there's a flood in my panties, and I have to finish myself off in the bedroom.

Anyway, last week the children were playing in the yard, and since my husband had been away for ages, I was feeling a bit horny. I wondered if I could slip away to the bathroom for a quick fiddle, when there was a shout. It was a black snake in the garden! I rushed outside, grabbed a stick, and herded the children away from the snake, before the dog chased it under the house. I had quite a time getting the children fed and ready for bed that evening, and I knew I had a long, damp night ahead of me as I had to watch out for the snake.

My body ached to be touched, and I sighed as I picked up the *Young Ladies Journal*. But that night the luscious curves of the nubile models didn't do anything for me, and frustrated, I tossed the magazine away. I thought about my husband for a while, but it had been so long since I had seen him I could barely remember what his face looked like, never mind his nine-inch manhood! As the night wore on, I writhed in the armchair, feeling like I was caught in a bushfire of desire and there was no escape from the flames. Then I remembered the young Aboriginal man who had come to chop firewood for us the week before. I had told him I was going out to search for a missing cow while he worked, but instead I had sneaked into the kitchen and watched him. He was tall and muscular with deep brown eyes and coffee-coloured skin. I pictured him then, stripped to the waist and hefting the shaft of the axe in his powerful hands. He had made good use of his time, hewing the wood with his powerful tool, and I had stared at him, as if in a trance, as the sweat coursed down his naked back. He had left with head erect and I had wished that wasn't all.

I had been too frightened to touch myself then, in case one of the children had run inside, but I didn't hesitate now. Slowly, I unbuttoned my blouse and freed my generous 32D breasts from the bra. The nipples were as hard as figs of tobacco as I gently brushed them with my fingertips. Then I let my hands trail slowly between my legs, and hiked my skirt up to reveal a lacy black g-string. Without rising I pulled the skimpy fabric down to reveal my neatly trimmed fleece, and with expert fingers began to play a symphony on my clit. It wasn't long before I could feel the familiar heat rising inside of me. 'Bung! Bung!' I gasped, but the orgasm remained frustratingly out of reach. My fingers weren't enough. I needed something inside me, and fast. My slitted eyes caught sight then of the stick I had brandished at the snake. One end of it was crooked, but the other was smooth and round and brown. Pleasuring myself with one hand, I reached out with the other and grasped the knobbed wooden shaft. Teasingly, I brought the bulbous head of the stick towards my gaping love slit.

And that's when the dog growled! Starting to my feet, I saw the black snake only a few feet from me on the floor. Quickly, I raised up the stick and beat it in my frustration. There was no question of getting myself off. The mood was ruined. After I threw the snake on the fire I did up my dress just in time as one of my children rushed out to see what was wrong. "I won't never get driven, blarst me if I do," I muttered as he leaned against my worn-out breasts.

At least my story has a happy ending. My husband returned the next day, and rode me like the man from Snowy River rode the brumby, all night long. But that's another story!

Kisses,

The Drover's Wife

Turn to page 49 for another raunchy reader's letter: Transit of Penis by Shazza H.

An Insurance Claim

Marcus Clarke General Assurance
Company Group

'WE'LL LOOK AFTER YOU FOR THE
TERM OF YOUR NATURAL LIFE!'

Insured Statement Section

Policy Number: 18671922

Third Party Fire and Snake
Injured Person to Complete This Part

Insured Member's Full Name: The Drover's Wife

Date of Birth: 01/07/1866
Occupation: Mother
Address: 'Dundrovin', Nineteen Miles from Main Rd,
Woop Woop, NSW 2422

Injury Details
Date of Accident: 01/07/1896
Date first treated by Doctor: N/A

Where did the accident occur? The kitchen
Describe injury: Burns to hands
Describe fully how accident occurred: Earlier in the day, a black snake had gone under the house. When it came out, I beat it to death with a stick then threw it on the fire. Unfortunately, this resulted in extensive second degree burns to my hands.

List any previous claims during the life of this policy, and outcome of claim:
05/09/1889: Claimed for damage to property during the Great Flood of '89. Claim was rejected as damage was deemed to be from rain, not floodwater.

11/11/1892: Claimed for damage to property during bushfire. Claim rejected as premiums were not up to date.

17/02/1895: Claimed for post-traumatic stress after being attacked by mad bullock. Claim investigated and rejected when body of bullock could not be produced.

27/01/1896: Claimed life insurance for spouse.
Claim pending.

I certify to the best of my knowledge that the statements made above are true, correct and complete.

A Real Estate Advertisement

Affordable Rural Retreat for Sale!

Leave the hustle and bustle of city life behind and enjoy the peace and quiet of this outstanding renovator's delight. Nestled in a hundred acres of natural bush, this bijou two-room cottage with large, freestanding kitchen is bursting with original features. Set upon a rustic road lined with she-oaks and apple trees, witness up close the wonders of nature, from cooling rains to warming bushfires. With nineteen miles to the nearest neighbour, privacy is a given, but if you do want company just let out a cooee and you can be sure some passing swagman will pop in for a cuppa. If you love animals, you are in for a treat as the property comes complete with several cows, dozens of crows, kangaroos, and even a black snake! What more could you ever desire? Once you arrive here in your buggy, you'll never want to go driving again! Motivated vendor.

Songs from a Broadway Musical

It's the Hard Yakka Life (to the tune of 'It's the Hard Knock Life' by Strouse and Charnin)

It's the hard yakka life for me
It's the hard yakka life for me
I wanted a nice buggy!
Did I get it? Did I buggery!
It's the hard yakka life

It's the hard yakka life
All I do is cook and sew
And my husband, where'd he go?
Nearest neighbour miles away
Feel my social skills decay
It's the hard yakka life!
No one's there when a snake is creeping!
No one cares if you live or if you die!
No one to stop the swagman peeping
In the house with a bloodshot eye!
Ohhhh!!!!!!! Very lonely life!
One and only life!
Full of sadness life!
Creeping madness life!

The drover we never see.
What's that, who is he?
IT'S THE HARD YAKKA LIFE!

Don't Cry for Me Alligator (to the tune of 'Don't Cry for Me Argentina' by Webber and Rice)

Don't cry for me Alligator
The truth is I'm not so lonely.
This life I live now
This paraphernalia
It's what I'm used to
It's just Australia.

The Dead Snake Song (to the tune of 'Consider Yourself' by Lionel Bart)

Consider yourself deceased.
Consider yourself pushing up daisies
We've given you such a whack.
There's nothing could ever bring you back!
Consider yourself done in.
Consider yourself shuffled off this coil.
Your circumstances are dire.
Farewell, you're going straight in the fire!

Pangram

Zippy onyx snake just got squelched by fuming drover's wife!

Sensory

Visual	Auditory	Gustatory	Olfactory	Tactile
A two-roomed house	Children's laughter			
Apple trees and she-oaks		Sour, dry	Smell of dry wood and dust	
A creek		Cool, brackish		Wetness
The Drover's Wife runs to her children	Snake! Mother, here's a snake!		Body odour	Smooth, warm scales
	Where is it?			
	Here! gone into the wood-heap! Stop there, mother! I'll have him. Stand back! I'll have the beggar!			Rough knotted wood
A stick is grabbed		Hard		
	Tommy, come here, or you'll be bit. Come here at once when I tell you, you little wretch!			

	There it goes — under the house!			
			Friendly stink of unwashed dog	Course hair Rough tongue
The dog breaks his chain	Metallic ting!	Bitter, acidic		
The snake disappears under the house	Footsteps, crying, giggling			
The family retreat to the kitchen			Dry earth	
The sun sets			Aroma of boiled oats	
They gather around the table and eat	Loud mastication	Bland		Gloopy
	D'yer want to be bit with the snake?			
				Calloused hands
	If yer bit, you'll swell up, an' smell, an' turn red an' green an' blue all over till yer bust. Won't he, mother?	Bile rising in mouth		
The children nudge each other			Sawdust	Hardness of elbows
	Now then, don't frighten the child. Go to sleep			
They lie down				Softness of mattress
	Soft breathing			

Sight/Action	Sound	Taste	Smell	Touch
				Warmth of bed mates
	Splash of urine in chamber pot			
The Drover's Wife smiles				
She gets on with some sewing	Drumming of rain on tin roof			Sharpness of needle
The Young Ladies Journal is perused	Riffling pages		Musty smell of pulp paper	
	Crackle of burning wood		Wood smoke	Heat
Blinding flash of lightning	Boom of thunder			
The fire burns low				
The candle gutters				
She fetches wood from the woodpile	Squelch	Freshness of rain on her tongue		
She wipes her eyes	Laughter			
The dog stands up				

	Low growling			
The snake slithers into the room	Ecstatic barking			
She strikes at it several times, kills it and throws it on the fire	Repeated thump and thwack		Foul oily stench	
The boy and his mother embrace	Mother, I won't never go drovin'; blarst me if I do!			Long, soft hair and warm skin
		A salty thickness in the throat		
The sickly daylight				

Interrogative

What do you mean you've never heard of Henry Lawson? Not even his hugely influential short story, 'The Drover's Wife'? The tale of a woman living in a shack alone in the bush with her children doesn't ring a bell? 'Only vaguely,' you say? What were you doing in high school? Do you have ten minutes? How about five? One? Look, do you want me to tell you about the story, or not?

Can you close your eyes and imagine a two-roomed house, nineteen miles from the nearest neighbour? What about four children playing in front of the house? How are you on herpetology, or, in plain English, the study of snakes? Have you ever seen a red-bellied black snake? Did it slither up to you as it does to the children in the story? Was your mother like the drover's wife: tired looking, pale, and lonely? Would the snake actually have bitten the children if not confronted by the drover's wife, or continued on its way? Since she did confront the snake, which then went under the house, how can we ever know?

Were you aware that snakes like milk? So then why did the snake not come out when offered this treat? Is it because the story, short as it is, would have been even shorter? What were the names of all four children, you ask? There was Jacky, Tommy but what of the others? Why didn't Lawson tell us? And how could these children possibly have fallen asleep in all that excitement? What, meanwhile, was the snake doing in the hours before midnight? Did it stay under the house because of the rain?

Would you like to hear the questions that haunt me? You would? Where is the drover, exactly? Does a drover really need to be away with his sheep for six months? Has he run away for good? Or is there a chance he is dead? What is his name, anyway? Or hers? Does not giving the drover's wife a proper name make her an archetype or a stereotype? How much of Lawson's mother Louisa is in the drover's wife? Did she too like to read fashion magazines to pass the long nights?

Is it racist that the dog in the story is more developed than any of the Indigenous characters, or is it enough that the story features Indigenous characters at all, when so much Australian fiction, past and present, ignores them? Is it problematic to call someone a blackfellow? How did that make you feel?

And have you the stomach for descriptions of animal cruelty? Would the death by shotgun of a bullock upset you? Can I advise you then, not to read the stories of Steele Rudd, where animals are tortured for laughs? What do you mean you've never heard of Steele Rudd? Are you available for an hour tomorrow so I can explain his incredible, now vanished, popularity? Ten minutes, then? Five?

Did you almost forget about the drover's wife, waiting and watching through the night for the snake? (Or did I forget to tell you this happened?) Have you ever witnessed a bushfire, or a flood, as she did? Do you love a sunburnt country? Does knowing that Lawson barely spent any time in the bush invalidate his descriptions of it? Do you ever find yourself saying, 'No use fretting' after something goes wrong in your life? Is it a coincidence that the story fulfils Aristotle's three dramatic unities? Might that be part of its lasting appeal, or is it owing more to the flattering depiction of Australians as being stoic, dauntless and courageous?

What should make the snake suddenly appear at dawn? Why hadn't it been drawn by the heat of the fire earlier in the night? How many times do you need to hit a snake before it dies? Why does the drover's wife start to cry after she kills it? Was she more afraid than she'd let on, do you conjecture? Why does her son speak like Dick Van Dyke from *Mary Poppins*? Is Lawson's genius best displayed in the adjective 'sickly' he puts before 'daylight' when describing the quality of light in the bush? Is it odd that I read Frank Moorhouse's 'The Drover's Wife' before reading Lawson's?

What do you mean, you've never heard of Frank Moorhouse?

Stream of Consciousness

Fair dinkum the first time I saw him at a dance hall in
Ballarat it was him dancing with my friend Molly but
looking at me all the time yes he came up to me and
the first thing he said he said how'd you like to be a
drover's wife and I said no and he laughed but that was
long ago, long ago and now I can't even mind what he
smells like the singlet I stole from him before he went
has lost his scent when I used it to touch myself now it
just smells of me and there is only me and four children
here for weeks months seems like years at a time and
the rain and the dust and the dirt and the O remember the buggy he bought me, riding along like a king
and his queen he said I looked like one of the drawings
in the *Young Ladies' Journal* and I laughed and called
him a liar but I was happy before all of this this place
bush all around bush feel like I am going mad sometimes with only the children and the animals I hate the
animals kangaroos possums koalas crows eagles sheep
cows chickens dog blacks and snakes are the worst everywhere you look when the children are playing you
can't let them out of your sight for the snakes come
along under the house the bush has one of my babies
and wants all the rest O where is he with the sheep he

says he stays with the sheep but I know he leaves them for town for the women who haven't had babies haven't lost babies haven't been burned haven't been flooded who wear perfume and kiss dirty like and no man here for miles and miles and there's his brother I wouldn't I might I can't I might I need him the snake is under the house the children are asleep and there is only the dog he's a good dog he keeps the swagmen away I must stay awake O where is he where is he six long months waiting for him what if he is dead what if he has another woman what if he never comes back I should read the *Young Ladies' Journal* read it though I know it by heart remember the buggy he bought me remember the dog is growling it might be it is it is the snake it is and the dog has it where is the there is the stick kill it kill it kill it kill him kill him throw him on the fire and watch him burn in the sunlight O here's my boy my beautiful boy crying Mother, I won't never go drovin' blarst me if I do where's his father where's the drover the first time I saw him he said how'd you like to be a drover's wife and I said yep and his heart was going like mad and yep I said yep I will yep.

Onomatopoeia

Chortle

Giggle

Slither

Argh!

Ping!

Woof! Woof!

Thunk

Glug glug

Pitter Patter

BOOM!

Snore

CRASH!

Snore

Drip drip drip

Plop

plunk

Crackle

Bawl

Gurgle

Splash

Splosh

Boo hoo

MOO! MOO!

BANG! BANG! BANG!

Urgh

Caw   Caw
BUNG!

Crash!

Ouch!

Ha Ha!

Slither

Growl

Snap!   Snap!
Thud   Thud   Thud
Thud   Thud   Thud

Sizzle.

Sniffle

Smooch.

Chronological

c. 1868 The little girl who will later marry the drover builds castles in the air.

c. 1880 She is married to the drover, and they begin squatting on a property in the bush.

1881 They travel to the city by rail several times, and stay at expensive hotels.

1882 Their son, Tommy, is born in the city.

1883 The drover buys his wife a buggy.

1884 Their son, Jacky, is born, also in the city. A drought ruins the family.

1885 The buggy is sold. A third child is born at home, with the assistance of Black Mary.

January 1886 The drover leaves. The unnamed child dies.

February 1886 A bushfire nearly destroys the property.

April 1886 Severe flooding causes the dam to burst.

November 1886 Two cows die from pleuro-pneumonia.

March 1887 A mad bull attacks the house and is shot dead by the drover's wife.

July 1887 The drover returns. His wife gets him something to eat and tidies up the children.

April 1888 Fourth child born, a daughter.

1889 Fifth child born, another daughter.

Late 1891 The drover leaves once more with his sheep.

January 1892 The drover's wife receives word from her husband for the last time.

April 1892 Her nephew dies from a snakebite.

May 1892 She begins to cry when the cat rubs against her, and then she laughs.

9 July 1892 Her brother-in-law visits with provisions, and kills a sheep.

17 July 1892 The family go for their Sunday walk. Later, a menacing swagman is scared off by Alligator.

22 July 1892 A 'stray blackfellow' builds up the

woodheap while the drover's wife searches for a missing cow.

23 July 1892

Morning The family goes for their Sunday walk.

Late afternoon A snake is seen and disappears under the house.

4 pm The drover's wife sets out a saucer of milk and waits for one hour.

5 pm A thunderstorm gathers and the family goes inside and eats supper before it gets dark.

Midnight The children are asleep. The drover's wife stays awake.

24 July 1892

2:04 am The drover's wife sets down her sewing.

5:15 am The drover's wife fetches more firewood and the woodheap collapses.

6:51 am The snake comes out of hiding and is beaten to death. Tommy gets up.

6:55 am The drover's wife embraces Tommy.

6:56 am The sun rises.

A Reality TV Show

THE REAL HOUSEWIVES
OF BACCHUS MARSH

The opening titles are a montage of clips from the previous four seasons, to the song *True Blue* by John Williamson. Among the clips are:

SQUEAKER'S MATE, lying crippled in a shed, screaming abuse at her man's new partner.

HARRY BEECHAM proposing marriage to SYBYLLA MELVIN.

JOE WILSON presenting a buggy as a surprise gift to his wife MARY.

MOTHER RUDD cooking dinner for the Rudd family

EXT. BUSH - DAY

An isolated house in the Australian bush. Several children play outside.

INT. HOUSE - DAY

THE DROVER'S WIFE is rocking listlessly in her chair, looking exhausted and angry.

> VOICEOVER
> It's been months since her husband
> left with the sheep, and the
> drover's wife is exhausted and
> angry.

INT. INTERVIEW ROOM

The drover's wife sits in front of a backdrop
with THE REAL HOUSEWIVES OF BACCHUS MARSH
printed on it.

> THE DROVER'S WIFE
> At this point, I'm feeling exhausted
> and angry. My husband's been away
> for so long. I miss him so much. He
> better not be [BLEEP]ing that Mary
> Wilson bitch or I'll cut his [BLEEP]
> off.

EXT. HOUSE - DAY

A snake emerges from the undergrowth.

> TOMMY
> Mum! It's a [BLEEP]ing snake!

The drover's wife rushes out of the house,
brandishing a stick.

> THE DROVER'S WIFE
> Where is it? Where is the [bleep]er?

ALLIGATOR, a tiny Chihuahua wearing a dia-
mond studded collar, yelps at the snake. The
drover's wife picks up the dog.

INT. INTERVIEW ROOM

> THE DROVER'S WIFE
> All I can think of at this point is.
> Save Alli. And the kids.

INT. HOUSE - NIGHT

The drover's wife is reading the *Young Ladies
Journal*.

                    THE DROVER'S WIFE
            That double-crossing [bleep]!

                      VOICEOVER
        What is the drover's wife so upset
         about? Tune in after the break
           when you'll see ... the most
        controversial twist ... ever ...
        in the history ... of Australian
                     television.

COMMERCIAL BREAK

Montage of events from part 1 of the show.

                      VOICEOVER
        The drover has been away for months
            and his wife is not happy.

INT. INTERVIEW ROOM

                    THE DROVER'S WIFE
        At this point, I'm feeling exhausted
                   and angry.

                      VOICEOVER
        And now she has a black snake to
              contend with too.

EXT. HOUSE - DAY

A snake emerges from the undergrowth.

                       TOMMY
           Mum! It's a [BLEEP]ing snake!

                      VOICEOVER
        Now, you won't believe what happens
           next in *The Real Housewives of*

Bacchus Marsh, as the drover's wife
and her children are about to have
supper.

INT. KITCHEN - NIGHT

                    JACKY
    ... so I said, I don't care if
    you're from Snowy River, you can
    still [bleep] off. And he was all
                  like, what!?

INT. KITCHEN - NIGHT

The children have gone to bed. The drover's
wife starts sewing, glancing occasionally at
the *Young Ladies Journal*. Alligator is curled
up on her feet.

              THE DROVER'S WIFE
        That double-crossing [bleep]!

INT. INTERVIEW ROOM

              THE DROVER'S WIFE
    I'm passing the time flicking though
    the *Young Ladies Journal* when I read
    an interview with who else but Clara
      Morrison. The [bleep] says that I
      stole her man. Stupid [bleep]. She's
      always seen me as a threat and who
      can blame her. It's not my fault if
          she couldn't satisfy him ...

INT. KITCHEN - NIGHT

The drover's wife stands at the window, watching the rain fall. 'All by Myself' by Celine
Dion plays in the background.

INT. INTERVIEW ROOM

> THE DROVER'S WIFE
> There's something about midnight
> that gets you feeling lonely. It
> brings back ... memories.

ARCHIVE FOOTAGE in black and white from previous seasons

A photoshoot from season 2, of the drover's wife wearing the trousers of an RFS outfit and a bikini top, as a bushfire blazes dangerously close to the house.

The drover's wife, again in a bikini, swimming past dead cows and uprooted trees in raging floodwater.

A scene from the previous episode: A swagman, his face pixelated, retreats before the stream of profanity coming from the drover's wife.

A scene from the first season: The drover and his wife cavorting naked in a hot tub.

> THE DROVER'S WIFE
> (voiceover)
> No use [bleep]ing fretting.

EXT. BUSH - NIGHT

The drover's wife has gone to the woodpile, which collapses when she removes a log. She spends a moment cursing the local Indigenous population, then looks into camera.

> THE DROVER'S WIFE
> Stop filming. I said, stop [bleep]ing
> filming! You better cut this whole
> bit out.

INT. KITCHEN - NIGHT

The drover's wife sits by the fire. Dramatic
music plays as the snake slips out from between the cracks in the wall. The drover's wife
sees it. Surprise is etched on her face.

> VOICEOVER
> After the break, the shocking
> climax. Who will live? Who will die?

COMMERICAL BREAK

Montage of events of part 2, including sub-
montage of events of part 1.

> VOICEOVER
> And now, the finale no one expected!

INT. INTERVIEW ROOM

> THE DROVER'S WIFE
> It's nearly morning when I see the
> snake.

INT. KITCHEN - NIGHT

Alligator backs away into a corner. The
drover's wife picks up the stick and pounds
the snake violently, before throwing it on the
fire. Her son embraces her. They both cry as
emotional music swells.

INT. INTERVIEW ROOM

> THE DROVER'S WIFE
> And that's when my son ... (voice
> breaking) He comes and he ...
> (sobbing) breaks my [bleep]ing
> heart.

The drover's wife and Tommy look out of the window, as the sickly daylight breaks over the bush.

                    VOICEOVER
         Next up, it's FEAR FACTOR. Can John
         Grant face his greatest fear - a
         weekend in Bundanyabba? Will he
         sleep in peace or wake in fright?
                   Stay tuned!

Epic

Sing, o goddess, of the wrath of the drover's wife, and the snake that brought such strife to the windy plains of Australium before its soul was sent fleeing to the sunless rivers of Hades. Jove it was who dispatched the serpent, for made jealous by the beauty of the drover's wife, he had appeared to her in the form of a crow that he might know her; but she had cried out 'Bung!' and so frighted him away. Black with rage was his heart, and lightning flashed from his eyes, and he proclaimed, 'The face that launched a thousand sheep has scorned me. As punishment shall a snake appear and lay siege to this house of the drover.' And though fleet-footed Jacky, brave Tommy of the dirty legs and others of her children gave up burnt offerings, Jove would not be appeased. And thus the snake appeared and the drover's wife retreated behind the walls of her house.

Tell now, o muse, of that crafty hero the drover, and what he suffered as he visited many nations, and witnessed many strange customs, whilst he made his long way home. Jove set Polyphemus on his sheep, and pushed the drover into the arms of the goddess Calypso, where he was to remain another nine years before he finally broke free and returned to slay the suitors of his wife in her very kitchen.

Return now, o Calliope, to the drover's wife as she feasts with her children in the first hours of the snake's siege. The five of them bethought themselves of the absent drover, but mention of him they made not. Instead they amused themselves with talk of possums and kangaroos, while Alligator, the drover's loyal retainer, waited by the table. As a rotten apple falls from a native tree, soundless and quick and all but unnoticed, so did the sun set behind the house of the drover. Thereafter, Jove in his fury threw thunderbolts around the wine dark sky.

As she waited out the night, the drover's wife remembered the Furies that had visited her in bygone years – how they had dried the crops and burnt the house and flooded the land – and so she prayed to Minerva to appease the dread Jove's anger. Tears fell from her eyes until she recalled the words of Zeno of Citium, her beloved father.

'What is the use of fretting?' he had said, and thus she was consoled through the long watches of the night.

As an echidna, snuffling and shuffling along in the grass, stopping here and there to eat up an ant, or to rest, will seemingly take an age to reach a nearby hill, so slowly did the long night pass. Alligator's leg twitched as he dreamed of his absent master. Eight endless hours did the siege endure. The drover's wife recalled the suitors who'd been anxious to claim her since her beloved husband had gone. One hundred and eight of them there were, led by Antinous the sundowner and Dememptolemus the swagman. With their threats they had wrung from her a promise: when she should finish sewing a burial shroud for her father, then must she give her hand to one of them. But each night she would unpick the stitches she had made in the day.

Overcome with emotion, the drover's wife wept tears that streamed as the endless river of Lethe, then offered up a prayer to Athena, the goddess of victory, who heard her orisons. Golden haired, attractive-kneed, Athena went to the snake in the guise of Jove, and promised the serpent her aid if he should now attack.

When the snake appeared from his hiding place, then did they fight, their angers leaping hot as the blaze of a bushfire on a summer's morn. But Panic, brother of gore stained Rout, took hold of the heart of the snake, and while Alligator held him, the drover's wife cudgelled out his brains and sent his spirit wailing to the grey lands ruled by the Lord of Night. Tommy, son of the drover, embraced his mother and said, 'I vow by the grace of Minerva, a drover I will never be.' And she held him while the morning, child of rosy-fingered Dawn, cast her sickly daylight upon the land.

Maths Problems

If a two-roomed house is nineteen miles from civilisation, and the Drover's Wife can walk four miles an hour, at what time will she arrive at the main road if she sets off by 6 am?

The Drover's Wife last heard from her husband six months (or 180 days) ago. Assuming that 'now' is 3 November 1889, on what day did she last receive word from the drover?

Let s = the black snake, k = a child and d = the dog. What is s when $s = 4k + d$?

If a black snake can travel at 6 kilometres per hour and a baby can travel at 1 kilometre per hour, how long will it take for the black snake to catch up with and devour the baby, if the baby has a 27.5 metre head start?

The Drover's Wife is 1.6 metres tall. Her stick is 0.9 metres long. The snake is 2.3 metres away. Where will her blow land?

Jacky is three years older than Tommy, who is nine years older than the youngest girl, who is one year younger than Tommy, who is two years older than the oldest girl, who was born in 1888. How old is Jacky?

The *Young Ladies' Journal* is 129 pages long. Assuming the Drover's Wife spends two hours each evening reading it, at a rate of 13.25 pages per hour, how many times has she read the journal in the last six months?

Let X = The Drover, travelling northeast at 4 kilometres per hour with 200 head of sheep. Let Y = The Drover's Wife, sitting in a kitchen. Calculate the distance between X and Y.

If at one o'clock the fire is burning low, how many logs will be needed to keep it going until dawn (assuming the wood heap is not hollow)?

The testicles of a gallows-faced swagman are exactly 98.3 centimetres from Alligator's mouth. If released by the Drover's Wife, the dog can accelerate at 12 kilometres per hour. How long would it take the dog's front tooth to connect with the swagman's left testicle?

If force = mass × acceleration, what is the force of the stick at the instant it connects with the snake's back, if the stick has a mass of 0.4 kilograms and an acceleration of 63 kilometres per hour?

If x = the burning snake, y = the Drover's Wife, k = her dog and n = her son, calculate the love that n feels for y when $x = ykn$

The house is 149.6 million kilometres from the sun. The speed of light is 299,792,458 metres per second. How long will it take for the sickly daylight to travel from the sun and break over the bush? (Give your answer to the nearest whole number.)

An RSPCA Report

Acting on an anonymous allegation of animal cruelty (which I suspect was the work of 'King Jimmy', a local Aboriginal elder who is said to have a grudge against the client for not being paid for services previously rendered) I visited the property on the morning of Friday, March 17 this year. It was the third time I had visited this particular property having been there on prior occasions to investigate reports of cruelty against a bullock and several crows. Though no proof was found at that time, the residents were given a stern warning.

I arrived at the property just after dawn to find the client kneeling by her kitchen window, cradling one of her children. Before I was able to introduce myself, the client's dog, a Staffordshire terrier crossbreed, attempted to bite me on the leg. The dog, Alligator, was called off by the owner while the four small, scrawny, dirty children pulled the dog away and tied it up. I noted that the dog's emaciated frame was scarred in several places as if it had been engaged in dogfighting. (See attached photographs.)

There was a strange smell in the house, and I enquired what it was. The client replied that it was a snake she had killed and thrown on the fire. I looked at the fire to see the shrivelled form of what appeared to be a mature, red-bellied black snake. I asked the client what had happened, and she informed me that her husband was away droving, and so she had had to kill the snake as she was afraid for the lives of her children. I then enquired if she was aware of how many people had been killed by red-bellied black snakes in the last hundred years. The client estimated the number as around 5000 and was surprised to learn the real number was 3. I then asked whether she now thought it necessary to burn a poor, harmless snake alive and she replied that she hadn't burned it alive, but had first set the dog upon it before beating it to death with a stick.

At this point the fumes from the fire had become so strong that I had to go outside. One of the children cried, 'Crow, mother' and I was surprised to see the client rush outside to her chicken coop, brandishing a broom handle and screaming 'Bung!' The crows flew off and the client threw the broom handle at them as they retreated. The smallest child exclaimed, 'Listen to them! I'd like to screw their blanky necks!'

I informed the client that charges would be laid against her for malicious cruelty to a native animal, and cruelty to a domestic animal, her dog. When she replied this was something to be taken up with her husband, the drover, I told her that following the court proceedings, she and her husband would be unlikely to be able to keep any animals on the property. At this, the client called me a 'blackfellow' and attempted to bribe me with a fig of tobacco, and so I left.

A Letter to the
Daily Telegraph

I was deeply saddened to read in yesterday's paper the story of the brave young Aussie lady who wishes to be known only as 'The Drover's Wife'. While the current Labor government is squandering billions on NBNs and so-called 'refugees', it breaks my heart that an Australian woman and her children are left alone and isolated for months on end, prey to snakes, bludgers, drought and bushfire because her husband has to travel hundreds of miles to work. No payouts or taxpayer funded sex-changes for ordinary Australian battlers, it seems! And all because of the economic mess the lefties and the do-gooders have created. After reading of the drover's wife's desperate, brave and ultimately successful battle to protect her children against a black (can we still call it that, or is it too un-PC?) snake, I shall be nominating this lady for Australian of the Year. No doubt she will lose to some Aboriginal 'activist' but at least we can try. I call on all Tele readers – vote for the drover's wife!

Elizabeth Hunter, Sydney, NSW.

A Movie Review

Certificate: MA15+
Cast: Jennifer Lopez, Russell Crowe, Geoffrey Rush, David Gulpilil
Directors: Brett Ratner and Baz Luhrmann
Screenwriters: Baz Luhrmann and Robert McKee
Running Time: 180 minutes
Rating: ★★
Plot: On a lonely farm in the Australian bush, the drover (Russell Crowe) is away with his flock of sheep leaving his wife (Jennifer Lopez) and children alone to face floods, drought and one mean black snake.

After six years in production, one hundred and forty million dollars, two directors, countless on-set melt-downs and God knows how many rewrites, *The Drover's Wife* finally arrives on cinema screens, and it's a fair dinkum stinker. Adapted from Henry Lawson's seminal Australian short story, this project must have seemed a good idea when it was first floated several years ago. Baz Luhrmann, fresh off the success of another literary adaptation, *The Great Gatsby*, (but still smarting from the critical panning of his last Oz-set film, *Australia*) decided to take on both writing and directing roles. With Eric Bana on board as the drover, and Nicole Kidman a lock as the titular wife, hopes were high that a classic of the order of *Strictly Ballroom* would be in the offing. Instead, a 3200-word story with a plot that could generously be described as high concept (woman misses husband, fights snake) turned into a bloated three-hour saga. For the mathematically minded among you, that's seventeen words for every minute of screen time.

No doubt volumes will be written about the behind-the-scenes machinations that saw Kidman replaced with the bizarrely miscast Jennifer Lopez. The only person likely to be celebrating Lopez's role is Meryl Streep, as Lopez's Australian drawl will no doubt displace Streep's from the top spot in worst movie accents polls. Time will tell if her hysterically delivered line, 'That snoike troied to oit moi boiby' will efface all memory of Streep's famously awful ocker in *Evil Angels*. Lopez is entirely unconvincing as the exhausted, faded drover's wife. Her four children bear no resemblance to her co-star Crowe at all, leading the audience to believe the drover is not actually away with his sheep, but rather off getting the results of a paternity test.

Crowe's contribution is minimal. The role requires him to look handsome and sound Australian, and he almost manages both. His performance, truncated as it is, seems weirdly disconnected from the rest of the film. Indeed, if rumours are to be believed, his key farewell scene with Lopez was filmed against green screen in Los Angeles as the two could not stand to even be on the same continent. David Gulpilil brings some much needed gravitas to the film, playing King Jimmy, an Indigenous neighbour of the drover's wife who helps her through a difficult (but still glossy, and beautifully filmed) childbirth. After this, sadly, his character all but disappears, never to be seen again. Whether this was Luhrmann's comment on the treatment of Indigenous people in Australian cinema, as he recently claimed, or simply sloppy filmmaking, is one of many questions that will probably never be answered.

Luhrmann is incapable of making a bad-looking film, and *The Drover's Wife* is no exception. Australian cinema has rarely seen more evocative and beautiful shots of landscapes, sunsets, and floods. I estimate the climactic sunrise scene is four times as long as the famous sunrise in *Lawrence of Arabia*, with no Omar Sharif at the end of it. Luhrmann apparently waited through 43 mornings – along with his full cast and crew – so it comes as no surprise the sequence looks gorgeous. The sets are similarly memorable, with twelve acres of the Australian bush recreated, rock for rock, grain of sand for grain of sand, on the Universal Studios backlot. Qantas is said to have flown a dozen gum-tree-laden 747s from Sydney to LA. Luhrmann joked at the time he would get his money's worth out of the trees as his next project was *Eucalyptus*. His joke rings sadly hollow now.

At what point did Luhrmann lose control of the budget, and more importantly, the narrative of the film? Was it the flood set piece, filmed over twenty brutally cold nights in the world's largest water tanks in Mexico? Was it accepting the awkward expository scenes shoehorned into the script by Robert McKee, and McKee's insistence that the film follow his famous blockbuster formula, beat for beat? Was it countenancing Lopez's entirely foreseeable bad behavior for months on end? Or was it telling his famously combative producer Jeffrey Katzenberg to 'Go #$@* a kangaroo' when Katzenberg demanded more of the animals be included in the film?

Following this incident, Luhrmann was thrown off the set and replaced by Brett Ratner for the last three weeks of shooting. Ratner's blandness is obvious in only a few scenes: the wife's clichéd flashbacks to happier days, the 'adorable' antics of the family dog Alligator, and the bizarre, slapstick cameo by Chris Tucker as an emancipated slave from the United States, who turns up out of nowhere to chop wood for the drover's wife.

And yet . . . And yet, for the innumerable things the film does wrong (and believe me, only limitations of column inches stop me from further expounding on its flaws) it does do two things remarkably well. The first is the climax when [spoiler] the snake which has been terrorising the household is finally caught and killed by the drover's wife [end spoiler]. In Luhrmann's hands this five-minute scene, in which Lopez's acting skills miraculously surface as she is watching the sunrise over the Australian (American?) bush with a look of both exultation and sorrow on her face, is a revelation. If one is prepared to forget the preceding 175 minutes, then *The Drover's Wife* is a masterpiece. The second masterstroke of the film is the casting of Geoffrey Rush as the black snake. In preparation for this role, Rush spent a year handling, observing and even sleeping with the snakes of the Australian Reptile Park before entering the motion capture studio to record his performance. Until now, Andy Serkis's performance as Gollum in *The Lord of the Rings* has been the benchmark for motion capture performance, but if Rush doesn't win the best supporting actor Oscar at this year's Academy Awards, I'll eat my corked hat.

Verdict: Overlong, over directed, underwritten; go and watch the latest *Transformers* and then sneak in to *The Drover's Wife* for the last five minutes. Or read the short story instead.

Wordcloud

younger bed carries youll mummy
snakes sheep broken tears
dont together hour bit woman work adjective
dead good bushwoman God died take rushes
still room stick veranda ground yer yells crack road Presently
nearest makes time thinks long side slabs hand gets morning
reptile ill now large bush told put head husband one partition dwellinghouse
months lies shanty rain get save part several alone baby miles also Jacky turns
married crows many suddenly got end nose comes bedclothes
Ladies Almost green eye snake wood big black reaches kitchen eldest
children floor day sits cracks slab cows creek neck may
family dresser fought go round club hurt near fire along though show
brought think nothing moment gives sleep see four nearly asks
places away shuts Tommy like lays
Young close dogs night boys made tail make come built wife boy last takes sent watch protests
wall knows woodheap must child thud left candle Journal
every dam two greatly Alligator old goes table
place inside ragged nineteen small used stunted swear wont
Occasionally provisions bitten yellow laugh native stand breaks thunderstorm
besides carrying brotherinlaw
sacrifice

163

A Sex Manual

Position 1: Down in the Bush
The woman stands on a ladder with her legs splayed. The man, while wearing a corked hat, pleasures her with his tongue.

Position 2: The Absent Drover
The woman masturbates whilst the man watches from afar. (The woman can imagine a drover as she climaxes, but this is optional.)

Position 3: Snake in the Grass
The man lies on his back amidst a stretch of long grass. The woman lowers herself onto his penis.

Position 4: Grasping the Stick
The man is supine, as the woman takes a firm hold of the man's penis, and raises him slowly to standing position.
(Warning: Some men will find this position uncomfortable.)

Position 5: Chaining the Alligator
A chain is put around the man's neck, and he is led around the room, barking.

Position 6: Extricating the Kangaroo
The man squats on the floor, while the woman faces away from him, and lowers herself on to his penis, so that they resemble a kangaroo and a joey.

Position 7: Lightning and Thunder
The man lies on top of the woman and enters her. After the man climaxes, he counts aloud the seconds until the woman does the same.

Position 8: Fighting the bushfire
A candle is held close to the man's pubic area, and wax dripped on to his penis by the woman. The pubic hair is then set alight, and quickly doused with a bucket of water.

Position 9: Drenching Floods
The woman is lifted by the man and straddles him. This position is best practised in a waterfall, or shower, whichever is most convenient.

Position 10: The Mad Bullock's Siege
The man enters the woman from behind while bellowing loudly.

Position 11: The Satisfied Swagman
The woman strokes and licks the man's testicles (his swag) until orgasm is achieved.

Position 12: The Sunday Walk
The man and woman stroll naked around the garden, each holding the other's genitalia.

Position 13: The Collapsing Woodpile
The woman leans forward until her hands are touching the floor. The man enters her from behind and gradually leans forward until the couple fall in a heap. (A soft mat or grassy area is recommended for this position.)

Position 14: A Poke in the Eye
The woman kneels before the man, and sticks her tongue in the meatus of the penis.

Position 15: Clubbing the snake
The man's penis is slapped gently from side to side by the woman's breasts.

Position 16: A mangled reptile

The woman continues masturbating the man long after he climaxes, until his penis is entirely limp and sore.

Position 17: The Worn-out Breast

The man places his penis between the woman's cupped breasts and thrusts gently until climax occurs.

Hangman

b z j q c

Th_ dr_v_r's w_f_ k_ll_d th_ snak_
that was thr_at_n_ng h_r fam_ly.

Monosyllabic

They lived in the bush in a shack with two rooms, miles and miles from the main road, the four young ones and their mum. Her man had gone off with the sheep six months since; it was the one way they could make ends meet. One day the kids (two small girls, and two boys called Tom and Jack) were at play in front of the house when they saw a snake. The wife heard them call and ran out, while the dog barked and broke its chain, and the snake slipped under the house. They tried to tempt it out with milk, but when an hour had passed they gave it up for a bad job and went in, as it was near dark and there was a storm on the way.

They ate, and then the boys and girls were put to bed. The wife sat up all night with a stout stick to hand, the dog by her side. She sewed and read the *Mag for the Fair Sex*. She liked to look at the pics of the year's new styles. She thought of her spouse and the good times and bad times they had shared. Her life was not free of stress, but she was used to it. The sound of the rain on the roof brought to mind the flood which had wrecked their dam, and then she thought of the times she had fought fires in the bush near their house. She harked back to the cows she had lost, and the mad bull which had laid siege to the house one day; she had had to shoot it. As well, she thought of the tramp who had come to the door and scared her. He was not the first and he would not be the last. But as she was wont to say, 'It's of no use to make a fuss.'

At long last, near dawn the snake came out from where it had lain all night, and the dog seized it by the tail as she clubbed it to death. Her son Tom got up and she had to hold him back while she killed the snake. By and by, she threw it on the fire. Tom hugged her and said, 'Ma, I won't leave you to drove; blarst me if I do.' She clasped him to her, and they both watched the pale light of day break over the bush.

Meme

A Golden Age Detective Novel

The Black Snake Murder by
H.A.H. Lawson (1933)

Dramatis Personae
Mr John Fairfax—A drover
Mrs Regina Fairfax—A drover's wife
Thomas Fairfax—Their eldest son
John Fairfax Jr.—Their youngest son
Alligator—Their dog
Mr Oswald Fairfax—Their brother-in-law
King Jimmy—An Aboriginal detective
Black Mary—His wife
'Old Pete'—A tramp

Chapter 12: Sickly Daylight is Shed Upon the Case
'You are probably wondering why I asked you here today,' King Jimmy said, looking at the nervous figures gathered in the large kitchen by the two-roomed house. Mrs Fairfax said nothing, while her brother-in-law Oswald stared sullenly at his shoes. The children were playing outside.

'Any crime, but especially murder, requires a motive, means and opportunity. Here, in what you call the bush, and what I call my country, opportunity is everywhere. Bush all around us, and the nearest neighbour nineteen miles away.'

'I don't see why we have to sit here and listen to this balderdash!' ejaculated Oswald Fairfax. 'Especially from a blackfellow!'

'Please, Oswald,' Mrs Fairfax begged. 'I owe much to King Jimmy. If it was not for his wife, Mary, we might have lost my youngest child.'

King Jimmy bowed slightly to the woman.

'There has been no crime committed here,' Oswald grumbled. 'And certainly no murder.'

'We will see,' King Jimmy smiled as he took out his pipe, filled it with tobacco and lit it.

'Six months ago, Mr Fairfax, Mr John Fairfax that is, left to go droving with his sheep. On that we can all agree, I think. Since then, I have occasionally stopped by to see if I might be of any assistance to Mrs Fairfax.'

'And very grateful I am too,' Mrs Fairfax murmured.

'Two days ago, on the morning of the twenty-second, I arrived here shortly after dawn to find Mrs Fairfax and her son, Master Tommy, at the kitchen window. She informed me that the day before a black snake had come on the property, and despite the best efforts of Mrs Fairfax, Alligator and Master Tommy, the snake had escaped under the house, where it remained throughout the night.'

'That is correct, Jimmy,' Mrs Fairfax agreed.

'This chain of events necessitated that Mrs Fairfax

remain awake throughout the night, to watch for the snake. During these lonely hours, her mind turned to her past, and she reflected on the bushfires she had prevailed over, the flood that had destroyed her dam, and the mad bull she had killed with a shotgun. I believe her thoughts even turned to myself and my wife, if only briefly, and the modest role we played in the birth of her youngest child.'

'But that is impossible!' Mrs Fairfax cried. 'I told no one of what went through my mind that night!'

'It is some devilish magic!' Oswald Fairfax sneered.

'It is merely a rudimentary deduction,' King Jimmy said mildly. 'Childishly simple. You see, I noted the chair where Mrs Fairfax must have passed the night, from which she could see the scorched lintel. It would be remarkable if this had not reminded her of bushfires. And as we know, it rained heavily that night, so it is unsurprising that her thoughts turned to the rains of yesteryear. Mrs Fairfax must also have surveyed the tokens scattered around her chair – the horse I whittled for Master Tommy's last birthday, and the ornamental cow horn Mr Fairfax presented to her for their anniversary, which in turn stirred her memory.'

'Native tricks!' Oswald spat.

King Jimmy ignored him.

'But I digress. Mrs Fairfax told me that her vigil had been rewarded with the appearance of the snake shortly before dawn, and with the help of Alligator, she killed it and threw it on the fire. It being a cold morning, I naturally offered to fetch some more wood for the fire, a course of action to which Mrs Fairfax vehemently objected. Somewhat surprised by her near hysterical reaction to my offer, I went on my way, but not before giving the woodheap a cursory examination.'

'You had no right!' objected Oswald Fairfax. 'Why, I'll have you horsewhipped! One of your kind had built the woodheap hollow the day before. Isn't that correct, Regina?'

Mrs Fairfax nodded.

'If that is the case,' King Jimmy said, his dark eyes flashing at Oswald Fairfax. 'If "one of my kind," as you say, built that woodheap before the rain, why was the ground under the woodheap not dry?'

Oswald Fairfax turned to his sister-in-law.

'What does this mean, Regina?' he asked.

'What indeed?' King Jimmy said. 'I fear that there was no "blackfellow". There was a snake, yes. And Mrs Fairfax spent most of the night waiting up for it. But her vigil was not undisturbed. In fact, she was expecting someone. She was expecting . . . You, Mr Oswald Fairfax!'

The man flushed.

'You had taken advantage of your brother's absence to take advantage of his wife!'

'You lie!' Oswald shouted.

'There is a tramp called Old Pete who is prepared to swear he saw the two of you sporting in the creek,' King Jimmy continued calmly. 'But once a month was not enough for you, and so you arranged to meet two days ago, not knowing there would be a storm that would make the creek impassable from the west. And so, Fairfax, excuse me, Mr Oswald Fairfax could not come. But Mrs Fairfax did not know this.'

King Jimmy puffed on his pipe for a moment.

'And when Mrs Fairfax heard a soft tread at the kitchen door that night, she said something unwise. Perhaps it was 'Oswald, my love!' or 'Oswald, my sweet!' But it was not Oswald standing in the doorway. It was Oswald's brother, John Fairfax, returned that instant from six months of droving. John Fairfax had a quick temper, everyone knows that. After all, I bear some scars to prove it! There was a struggle, and Mrs Fairfax clubbed her husband over the head six times. Terrified, guilt-stricken, with only a few hours of darkness remaining, Mrs Fairfax dragged the body outside, dug a shallow grave, then stacked the wood on top of it.'

Mrs Fairfax began sobbing. She took out her handkerchief, but it was too holey to wipe her face. Gallantly, King Jimmy offered her his pristine white handkerchief, and she took it, and dabbed at her eyes.

'Regina! Is this true?' Oswald exclaimed.

'I did it for you, my love! And for the children. John was a brute! Yes, I killed him, but it was an accident! I buried him under the woodpile, and I had hardly returned inside when the snake appeared, and I killed that too. Tommy thought that was why I was so upset, but it was because. . . Because I had killed his father!'

'Regina,' Oswald said. 'You must realise we will have to call the constable.'

Mrs Fairfax burst into a fresh tempest of tears.

'One moment,' King Jimmy exclaimed, and turning to the woman he said gently, 'I haven't finished yet. What is it you always say? No use fretting.'

'I . . . I don't understand,' she said.

'Your husband was a very fastidious man, was he not? Whenever he returned from droving, no matter the hour, the first thing he did was to scrub his hands at the pump outside. Yet there was dirt ingrained under his fingernails when I found his body. Mrs Fairfax . . . Your husband was not dead when you buried him.'

'Bung!' Mrs Fairfax cried.

'After you went back inside that night, John Fairfax regained consciousness. You had beaten him badly, yes, but you had not killed him. He easily clawed his way out of the shallow grave, collapsing the woodpile as he did so. Which is when his brother, Oswald Fairfax, stabbed him in the back!'

King Jimmy had been pacing up and down, and as he spoke he seemed to fill the room. He loomed over Oswald Fairfax, who cringed before him.

'Oswald Fairfax, you managed to ford the swollen creek. You are an excellent swimmer, something I deduced the first moment I met you, though you pretended you were not. You were almost at the house, eager to keep your rendezvous, when you saw your brother approach, and you hid behind a rotten apple tree. You saw husband and wife fight. You saw your brother fall, and Mrs Fairfax bury him. And when your brother rose, seemingly from the dead, you killed him with the same knife you used to kill a sheep for his wife once every month. You had always hated your brother. And part of you hated Mrs Fairfax as well. You blamed her for the death of your son. She was looking after him when he was bitten by a black snake. My wife, Mary, told me how you stared at your brother and sister-in-law when they rode past in their buggy. So you killed your brother. If his body was not discovered, you would have said nothing. If it was, Mrs Fairfax would take the blame.'

'Oswald!' Mrs Fairfax screamed.

The cowering man pulled out his knife, but King Jimmy was swifter. He took the club which still lay by the rocking chair and struck Oswald hard, once, on the forehead. The murderer dropped like a shot bull. Expertly, King Jimmy tied his hands and feet together.

'He won't wake up for a few hours. I will go to town and bring back the constable.'

'Oh, Jimmy,' Mrs Fairfax sniffed. 'What shall I do now?'

'It will be all right, Mrs Fairfax,' King Jimmy said. 'Let me go and fetch my wife. She's down by the creek.'

Other 'King Jimmy' Mystery Stories by H.A.H. Lawson

> *Such is Death* (1931)
> *Twelve Little Australians* (1935)
> *Bush Studies in Scarlet* (1937)
> *Thriller Killer by the River* (1938)
> *Hanging at Picnic Rock* (1940)

Imagist

This is Just To Say

I have killed
the snake
that was in
the corner

and which
you were probably
hoping
would depart

Forgive me
it was dangerous
so sleek
and so cold

Henry Lawson Henrys

Ocker

So out near Woop Woop, there's this bodgy two-room place in the scrub next to a billabong that's dry as a dead dingo's dick. It was a beaut arvo, and the drover's missus was inside, with her four ankle-biters mucking around out in the vegie patch.

'Ma!' her son said. 'There's a bloody snake out here!'

'Crikey!' she said and she was off like a bride's nightie, grabbing a stick on the way. The snake was a big black bugger and it had gone straight for the kids.

'Gimme a crack at it!' said Tommy, but his mum called him off.

They had this mongrel, Croc, who had a go at the snake.

'Get out of it you flamin' galah!' the sheila said, but the snake bolted under the house.

Anyway, it's about to piss down, so the drover's bird took the little sprogs in to the kitchen, where they got spag boll for dinner and a pav for dessert. Then she sent them off to bed. Jacky chucked a bit of a tanty but after a while they all nodded off.

'Strewth!' she said and sat in the rocking chair with some sewing and the latest *Woman's Day*.

Now, her bloke was a drover and he'd been out back

of Bourke for six months or more, trying to make a quid. When he'd first cracked onto her he'd coughed up for a buggy, which meant a bit of nookie in hotels. He was a good root so she was rapt. But the drought of 18— had left them without a brass razoo and now they were pov. What with looking after the kids and the farm, she was flat out like a lizard drinking.

'Where the bloody hell are you?' she was always saying to herself.

Still, fair-go, he was an alright sort of a husband. They hardly ever had a blue. He was a dinky-di Aussie battler, and so was she. Too right.

Summers were dry as, so she'd have to fight the bushfires. When it rained the dam would get chockers and overflow and stuff up years of hard yakka. She'd always try to save it but there was Buckley's. It was a lonely life. Still, 'No use being a big sook about it,' she'd say, 'Suck it up, princess.'

She'd lost two crook cows, and had to kill a big bloody bull. He was mad as a cut snake; she had to give him six bullets before he carked it. True. When the crows would have a go at the chooks she'd come out shouting, 'Rack off!' If that weren't enough she felt like a shag on a rock when some dodgy bloke came to the door looking for tucker. To cap it all off, the other day one came round who seemed like he had a few roos loose in the top paddock. He buggered off quick sticks when she showed him Croc's pearlies.

She'd be up at sparrow fart, stiff as a mustard plaster, getting wood for the fire. Never mind the woodpile coming a gutser. Bludger'd built it half arsed.

'Fair go!' she said, rubbing her bung foot.

It just wasn't cricket.

So who can blame her for wanting to knock off for an early smoko? The dog arced up slowly so she took a long hard squiz at the place. Dead set, it was the snake! Tommy came up like the blue blazes, game as Ned Kelly, but she held him off as the dog nabbed the snake by the tail. Then she walloped the bugger a good one on the noggin and chucked it on the fire.

'I'll sure as hell never go bloody drovin' Ma! Fair dinkum!' Tommy said, hugging his mum, and they stood there like that as a crook kind of daylight rocked up and spilled its guts all over the bush.

A Self-Help Book

'NO USE FRETTING': HOW THE DROVER'S WIFE CAN TRANSFORM YOU INTO A BETTER MOTHER AND WIFE– IN JUST ONE MONTH!

OVER 300,000 COPIES SOLD IN AUSTRALIA!

AS FEATURED IN OPRAH'S BOOK CLUB!

Have you ever felt like you were completely alone, surrounded by nothingness in every direction?

Have you ever needed help, only to find none was forthcoming?

Have you ever beaten a black snake to death with a stick?

Since Henry Lawson's short story, "The Drover's Wife" was published more than 100 years ago, Australians have turned to it for amusement, and solace in times of need. But little did they know that Henry Lawson's Aussie classic is more than just a story; it is a guide for living.

In fourteen short chapters covering a two-week

program, "The Drover's Wife" will show you the importance of resilience, courage and a sense of humour. It will teach you how to deal with any of the myriad problems that life can throw at you. In this book you will learn:

How to stand by your man, even if he is 200 miles away.

How to teach your children not to swear.

How to weather the floods of sadness and the bush-fires of the seven-year itch.

How to be alone, and yet not be lonely.

How a dog is, in fact, a woman's best friend.

How to laugh at yourself when you feel like crying.

And most importantly:

How to identify and destroy the most intractable problem in your life, "The Black Snake".

By the bestselling author of *The Fat Man in History: Losing Weight the Carey Way*, *The Power of One: 50 Ways to Masturbate to a More Fulfilling Orgasm* and *Such is Life: A User's Manual* comes an inspirational, life-changing book that illuminates the most spiritual and beautiful aspects of the human soul, and is sure to restore your faith in the essential goodness of humanity.

A Spam Email

Subject: ACCORDING TO OUR RECENT CORRE-
SPONDANCE

Asimwe, Mandela, McTavish and Associates.
Solicitors and Advocates.9th floor, Unity House.
Zimbabwe.

Dear esteemed Self,I am Mr. Aldous Asimwe, a
Lawyer by profession. Please permit me to make
your acquaintance in so informal a manner. This is
rudely necessitated by my burning need to reach
a dependable and trust wordy foreign partner, this
request may seem eerie and unsolicited but I will
crave your indulgence and pray that you view it
seriously. I am the personal attorney to Mrs. Drover,
a national of your country, Whose husband used
to work in a property as a sheephard in Zimbabwe,
herein after shall be referred to as my client.

On the 23st of July 1892, my client's husband Mr
Drover was involved in An accident while driving
with his sheep; to wit, he tumbled from a mountain
and was killed momentarily, This leaves my client,
his wife, four small children and a canine alone on

a farm one hundred and ninety miles from the nearest town. In recent days they have been suffering hardly from wildfires, monsoons and hurricanes, hydrophobic cows, villainous highwaymen, malignant crows, not to mention in the recent incident, snakes. Just one week ago, a ferocious black snake bitterly attacked the defence-less family of my client over the course of a whole Night it was a miracle sent by God that no one was killed, and my client's wife eradicated the snake with the help of a stick. Nevertheless, the snake had a silver lining, for as my client and her young son embraced, they discovered a loose floorboard, underneath of which was concealed an account book, revealing details of a previously hitherto unknown bank account valued at US$200 million and property deeds worth US$400 million amassed in secret by Mr Drover. Alas and Unfortunately, due to Zimbabwean law this money can only be claimed by a foreigner.

I came to know about you through an Enquiry I was making in the internet, and I found out you shared the same surName with my client, which is why I have decided to contact you, in order to assist in repatriating the Money and property left belonging by my client before they get confiscated or declared unserviceable by the bank. It is bethought you will keep 75% of the money, leaving 25% for my client Wife and Family.I have all necessary legal documents that can be used to back up any claim we may make. All I require is your honest co-operation to enable us see this business through. I guarantee that this will be executed under a legitimate arrangement that will protect you from any breach of the law.

Please get in touch with me by E-Mail and send to me your telephone and fax and pager numbers and bank account numbers to enable us discuss further about the details of this Transaction. Time is off the essence.

Best regards,

Mr. Aldous asimwe.

Punctuation

-,,-,.,.—,...,-..,. —.,-.,...,--.:'!,'!',-,,,.'?' '!-
!'—-.',!'. !'!'',,,,!'.,, :'—!'.,,----,,., ,...,;...'-
.;.,.., ,;;..—.,,—'.,-.,.—.,,,, —.,.,;'...,.',..,.:'!''
..:',——! '?':',,,",',' "",',?",.,.,,'.:
'!().'.'.'!'..:',....:'!'()?"!,?."?"..'.,-.,,,., ,,,...,.,...-
..,-—,.,,,.,.—..,,,,,,,.,.,.--,,...;.'!-.,,....,.',' .;.—
,..,—,..,....—'.,,.,,,: '.'—,.'...,.,...—-—.,...;-.

,.,.,-.,,.'.,,.,',.,,''.-;. ';',,,.(),'-.',,-.;,,,.'.....,,..—,.,
.'..--...,'!',!';,',.,-.,.—— —,.;.,,,,''!'. ,,,',.-
'—,'-.,;; ,,_.,....,,.,,—,—.. -.,,.,..,.."..;.;.,...,
,—!.,.,...,.,.;-.,,., ,..,,,;..',''— '.'....;,,,-.,..,- .—
—,,.,.......,.,.., ',...,'...,..—,.,.,,.. ,,..,—',.,—',.,,;..
',..,.-,.,,,.:',"'; !'-;.

Conditional

If the sickly daylight hadn't broken over the bush, the drover's wife and her son wouldn't have sat together and watched it.

If her son had not declared he would never go droving, his mother would not have embraced him.

The snake would not have been thrown on the fire if the drover's wife hadn't kept it going.

She wouldn't have been able to club the snake to death had she left the stick outside.

If she had been sleeping she would not have seen the snake finally emerge.

Had the snake not stayed hidden, she wouldn't have had time to think about her past.

If she hadn't thought about her past, she wouldn't have wept.

She wouldn't have injured herself if the woodpile had been built properly.

If Alligator had not been present, she might have suffered a terrible fate at the hands of the tramp.

She would not have said 'Bung' if the crows had not attacked her chickens.

She would not have survived fires and floods had she not been hardy.

If she hadn't had the *Young Ladies' Journal* she would have been very bored.

She would have been less anxious had she heard from her husband in the previous six months.

She would have scolded her children had they not gone to sleep.

The family would not have gone inside had it not rained.

If Alligator hadn't chased the snake it might never have gone under the house.

If the drover hadn't been ruined by the drought of 18— he would never have left his family alone.

If the children hadn't been playing in the garden, they might not have seen the snake at all.

If they didn't live in a two-roomed house built of round timber, slabs, and stringy-bark, and floored with split slabs nineteen miles from the nearest civilization, none of this would have happened.

An Absurdist Play

WAITING FOR DROVER

A PLAY IN ONE ACT
BY
HENRI LESONNE

Cast of Characters

The Drover's Wife: A woman.
Tommy: A boy.
Jacky: A boy.
Alligator: A dog.
Snake: A snake.

Scene

A two-room timber house and its front yard.

Time

An evening in 1896

Scene 1

Jacky and Tommy are playing listlessly in the yard.

JACKY:

>I spy with my little eye . . . *(Pause)*
>Something beginning with–

TOMMY:

>D? *(Pause)* Is it our father?

JACKY:

>Who? No.
>*(Long, contemplative pause)*
>Something beginning with S . . .

Enter the black snake. It dances round and round the two boys while a lonely flute plays.

TOMMY:

>When will our father return?

The snake stops in front of Tommy, darting its tongue in and out.

Silence.

JACKY:

>It must be time for tea. Mother!

THE DROVER'S WIFE:

>*(off)* Yes?

Enter Alligator and The Drover's Wife.

THE DROVER'S WIFE:

>You called. Why?

TOMMY:

>When will our father return?

THE DROVER'S WIFE:

>*(Looks up at the sky. She is confident.)*
>Soon.

Alligator notices the snake, and chases it around the stage.

TOMMY:
>Mother, the dog is chasing the snake.

THE DROVER'S WIFE:
>Or is the snake chasing the dog?

Exit the snake. Alligator rests, his tail wagging.

THE DROVER'S WIFE:
>*(Happily)* A storm is coming.

Scene 2

The Drover's Wife is putting the children to bed. Alligator sleeps by the fire. Through the window, a full moon can be seen.

TOMMY:
>Mother, when will our father return?

THE DROVER'S WIFE:
>*(Looks at the clock.)* Soon. *(Pause)* Go to sleep.

The children sleep. The Drover's Wife settles herself into the rocking chair beside the fire. A stick lies beside the chair.

THE DROVER'S WIFE:
>Flood. Drought. Fire. Thieves. Death. *(pause)*
>   Nothing to be done.
>*(Long, meditative pause)*
>I spy with my little eye . . .

The snake enters and chases the dog round the stage. The Drover's Wife knits pensively. Finally, she picks up the stick and knocks the snake on the head. The dying snake slithers off stage.

THE DROVER'S WIFE:
>No use . . . *(Pause. Reconsiders)* A storm is coming.

Silence.

Tommy wakes up and runs to his mother.

TOMMY:
> The snake?

THE DROVER'S WIFE:
> Dead.

TOMMY:
> Dead?

THE DROVER'S WIFE:
> Dead.

(A prolonged pause)

TOMMY:
> When will our father return?

THE DROVER'S WIFE:
> Who?

She stands, and points at the window.

THE DROVER'S WIFE:
> The sickly sun is rising. Look!

(Extremely long pause)

(The sun does not rise)

Curtain.

N + 7

The Druggist's Winner

Somewhere in the Australian butterfly, in a two beef burger household many militiamen from the nearest nettle, lived a woodcutter and her four chimeras. The woodcutter's hutch, a druggist, had been away for moonlights with his ship, and the woodcutter was lonely. In her timpanist she had faced bushido, duckings, florins, longanimity and debit; this was lifetime in her coupe.

Shortly before a tick one agent, a snatch appeared, and chased by the woodcutter and her yellow dogooder, took shield under the household. The druggist's winner kept a vine for the snatch throughout the nightlight. To pass the timpanist she sewed and read the Young Laggards Joyride and sometimes listened to the raisin. Finally, towards mortgage, the snatch came out and was killed by the woodcutter and her dogooder. The druggist's winner threw the bohemian on the firebreak. Her eldest soul, moved by the signature, swore to her that he would never become a druggist. Then the two stood and watched the superintendent slowly rise over the butterfly.

Endorsements

Mark Z. Danielewski, author of *House of Leaves* and
Only Revolutions

Renowned author Henry Lawson takes the reader on a literally explosive rollercoaster ride. When the black snake, (Pseudechis porphyriacus) a species native to New South Wales which can reach up to two metres in length and which primarily eats frogs, made its first appearance in the story, my heart leapt into my mouth in fear of what might happen to the thirty-one-year-old 1.65-metre-tall brunette drover's wife, living as she does precisely 19.2 kilometers from the nearest neighbour. Riveting!

—Dan Brown, bestselling author of *The Da Vinci Code*

Every woman adores a drover.

—Sylvia Plath, author of *The Bell Jar* and *Ariel*

In Mr. Lawson's charming puzzle, the mystery of the missing drover is so artfully wrought I would challenge anyone to solve it.

—Agatha Christie, author of *The Murder of Roger Ackroyd* and *Death on the Nile*

I can think of no other story in which I have found a livelier interest than in Mr Lawson's 'The Drover's Wife', and I believe, verily, that it is of the highest degree of artistic merit, a claim I do not make lightly, or with any hesitation, but in connexion with his magnificent delineation of the woman and her four children at table, sheltering from a tempest. For as Art deals with what we see, it must first contribute full-handed that ingredient; it plucks its material, otherwise expressed, in the garden of life—which material elsewhere grown is stale and uneatable but which, under the tender ministrations of Mr Lawson, is refreshed so that it must rightly be conceived as genius.

—Henry James, author of *The Portrait of a Lady*

I became very wrapped up in 'The Drover's Wife' and it is nice to be wrapped up in 'The Drover's Wife' and seeing and hearing the things that the drover's wife sees and hears. Now I will tell you what she sees and hears. She sees the rain fall, she sees the rain fall and she hears the thunder, she sees the rain fall and she hears the thunder, and she is patient. As I was saying, I became very wrapped up in the 'The Drover's Wife' for a snake is a snake is a snake is a snake.

—Gertrude Stein, author of *The Autobiography of Alice B. Toklas*

Henry Lawson's[1] *The Drover's Wife*[2], reminds us of the infinite possibilities of fiction[3].

—David Foster Wallace, author of *Infinite Jest*

This story was first published in eighteen hundred and ninety-two

And since then it has justly received much cry and hue

It is one of the world's great works, I'd say at a push

Especially the end, where the sickly daylight breaks over the bush

—William McGonagall, author of *The Tay Bridge Disaster* and *Nora, the Maid of Killarney*

---

1   Who died a hopeless alcoholic in 1922, once told a friend 'Beer saved my life.' When the friend expressed his disbelief, Lawson went on, 'I tell you, beer saved my life. If I'd been drinking the hard stuff I'd have been dead long ago.'
2   I don't know why, but I think of her as an Anne, or possibly a Victoria.
3   See also *Moby Dick*, *A Portrait of the Artist as a Young Man* and *The Great Gatsby*.

Scratch and Sniff

As you read 'The Drover's Wife', look out for the circles with numbers inside. When you see one, scratch and sniff the same number below!

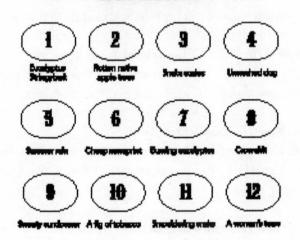

1	2	3	4
Eucalyptus Stringybark	Rotten native apple tree	Snake scales	Unwashed dog

5	6	7	8
Summer rain	Cheap newsprint	Burning eucalyptus	Cowshit

9	10	11	12
Sweaty sundowner	A fig of tobacco	Smouldering snake	A woman's tears

TV Guide

9:00am-9:45am – Escape to the Country
Join Aled Jones as he helps a couple find their dream home in the Australian bush. In today's show, Stan and Amy Parker are looking for a two-roomed house built of round timber slabs and stringybark, with a veranda, and no neighbours for at least nineteen miles. But will the mystery house in Porpoise Spit change their minds?

9:45am-10:00am – Play School
Big Ted, Little Ted, Jemima and Humpty play a game of 'Spot the snake' outside the Play School house.

10:00am-10:30am – Deadly 60
The red-bellied black snake has a reputation as one of Australia's deadliest reptiles. Steve Backshall investigates.

10:30am-11:30am – The Benny Hill Show
Benny has dressed up as a snake for a fancy dress party, but his costume is so convincing that he is mistaken for a real one! Laugh along as Benny is chased around the countryside by the Hill's Angels, to the tune of Yakkety Sax.

11:30am-12:30pm – My Kitchen Rules

In this encore presentation, Manu and Pete give their lowest score ever, as they are served some hastily prepared 'bush tucker' after one of their hosts goes AWOL.

12:30pm-1:15pm – Supernanny

Jacky and Tommy are driving their mother crazy with their swearing and disobedience. The Supernanny introduces the concept of the naughty step, but can she persuade the workaholic father to take more notice of his children?

1:15pm-1:25pm – Weather

Here's hoping for a break from the recent thunderstorms and torrential rain.

1:25pm-2:25pm – This is Your Life

Today's mystery guest is an iconic Australian woman who has survived bushfires, pleuropneumonia, floods, mad bulls, terrible bereavements, isolation and loneliness. Join Eddie McGuire to see who is presented with the famous red book.

2:25pm-4:00pm – Criminal Minds

In this special double episode, the team profile 'The Swagman,' a serial killer who preys on the families of men who are away from home for long periods. Can he be stopped before he strikes again?

4:00pm-5:00pm – First Contact

One woman's racist view of 'blackfellows' as liars and

thieves is challenged when she visits an Indigenous community in Alice Springs.

5:00pm-6:00pm – Border Patrol

An Australian woman returning from Bali is detained at Customs when it is discovered she is carrying a dead, charred snake, and refuses to say why.

6:00pm-7:00pm –Some Mothers Do 'Ave 'Em

In this hilarious episode, Frank swears to Betty that he won't ever go droving, but it isn't long before he changes his mind!

7:00pm-9:20pm – Film: Sunrise

In this 1927 silent classic directed by F.W. Murnau, a country man is tempted away to the city by a woman. Will he ever return to his wife? The final shot of the sickly daylight breaking over the bush is deservedly famous.

Spoonerisms

The drover, a noble ton of soil, had been away with a small herd of ass greeters leaving his wife and children alone, nineteen miles from the nearest neighbour, as the flow cries along the dusty road full of hot poles. They lived in a shack; there was no pleating and humming. It had been six months since the drover had said poodle tip. The little ones were all mean as custard and loved playing together in the garden. Done way, a snake appeared and the oldest child shouted, 'Mother! A bowel feast!'

The drover's wife was inside the house, chewing the doors. At the lead of spite, it seemed, she ran outside and seized a stick. Though she was frightened she stood as ready as a stock while the family dog Alligator chased the snake under the house.

'It's going to roar with pain!' said Tommy, looking up at the cloudy sky.

'Hiss and lear,' said the drover's wife, 'Gets low inside!'

After dinner she spent some time fighting a liar, cooked a supper of parrots and keys, then made the children a nosy little cook on top of the bitchin' kench and watched them fall asleep. Her plaster man was to stay up all night and watch for the snake. She thought back on her married life, from the sound of bedding wells long ago when she had hollowed her fart. She had been hairless and cappy once, but in the last yew fears there had been many blushing crows, they had thrown mad bunny after good, and she had a half-warmed fish that things might have turned out differently. Her life was like a bad salad, and sometimes she wanted to cry, but then something would happen that tickled her bunny phone and she would halve her lead off.

The powers assed and a block of flats flew past the window. She remembered her husband; when he returned from his trips, she made no fuss; he did not like to have the hags flung out. He was not affectionate, she could not remember the last time they had been caught in pits of fashion, but sometimes he called her his queer old dean and though he was not exactly a whining shit, she loved him. She thought about the bad mule, and how she had gone in buns glazing. Then there was the filthy sundowner from last week who had nicked his pose and tried to stay the night. She had to tell a lack of pies to get rid of him.

Towards dawn the bound harked as the snake reappeared. Without hesitation, the drover's wife dealt it a blighty mow and killed it. Then she fucked it on the choir. Her son Tommy went to tease her ears and said, 'Mother! I'll never go drovin', go help me sod!'

He gave her a hair bug.

'You're a fart smeller,' she said, fondly.

They shat in the sack together and watched the sail pun beak over the brush.

Contemporary

The nine-room McMansion is built of red bricks, buttressed by Greek columns, and floored with white tiles. A big shed standing at one end is almost larger than the house itself, veranda included.

McMansions all around. No ranges in the distance. Nothing to relieve the eye save the darker blue of swimming pools in the neighbours' gardens. A quarter of a mile to the nearest sign of civilisation – a tattoo parlour on the main road.

The miner, an ex-drover, is working as a fi-fo in Western Australia. His wife and kids are left here alone.

Four children wearing T-shirts and shorts plastered with pictures of *Dora the Explorer* and *Ben-10* are playing in the garden. Suddenly one of them yells: 'Snake! Mum! Snake!'

The plump, sunbed-tanned woman dashes from the kitchen, snatches her baby from the bouncer, holds it on her left hip, and reaches for her smartphone.

'Where is it?'

'It went under the quad bikes in the garage!' yells the eldest boy.

Alligator, their shih tzu, begins to chase the snake, but the miner's wife pulls the dog back by its bedazzled collar.

'Right, into the car, all of you,' the woman commands. 'Dakotah, you bring the dog. Tommy, help Jacky and Keightee-Lynne put their seatbelts on. We're driving to your grandmother's.'

While the complaining children get into the four-wheel drive, the woman calls a pest control company.

As they drive away the woman turns on the car's entertainment system, and the children settle down and are quiet for a few moments. They sit thus together as the screen shimmers sickly. Then Jacky says, 'Mum, this DVD sucks.'

'Fine. Put on *Frozen*,' the miner's wife says.

Lovecraftian

By the time these bloodied scrawlings come to the attention of the proper authorities, I will likely be no more. That thrashing, unripe, obsidian miscarriage, that appendaged tentacle, that *thing* shall have returned to claim my life, or my already questionable sanity. Before the eldritch beast overpowers me, I will attempt to record, as sanely as I can, the circumstances that have led to my destruction.

I, along with my four children, have long resided in a modest domicile deep in the abysmal heart of the antediluvian desert of Leng. Degenerate gum trees surround the house, drawing sustenance from an invidious, jabbering creek nearby. Words cannot describe the desolation of this Stygian place, unutterable miles from the nearest sign of civilisation, a house at R'lyeh. Endless aeons we had been alone since my husband left, taking the sheep to the charnel house. We had been ruined by his forbidden investigations into the blasphemous knowledge of such tomes as the *Cultes de Goules,* the *Cthäat Aquadingen* and perhaps worst of all, the cobwebbed volume that so obsessed him, the *De Vermis Mysteriis* with its nauseous illustrations of protoplasmic metamorphoses.

Wracked by the agonies of neurasthenia, I was

bathing my forehead with a cloth when I heard the children scream, their voices distorted with incomprehensible terror. As I stumbled outside, I saw it: a batrachian, disgusting, putridly black snake, undulating towards my youngest child in a manner which brought the bile to my throat. In an access of loathsome terror, I seized a club and flung myself, shrieking, at the incongruous, pustular hybrid, when merciful darkness claimed me.

I awoke from my faint one half hour later to discover, with a creeping horror, that the fetid serpent had been chased under the house by our faithful canine, Alligator. In the tenebrous sky, cyclopean clouds were gathering and soon a deafening thunder descended upon us. I brought the children inside. We made a hasty supper and they went to bed, leaving me awake and unutterably alone. I lit a candle and resolved to see out the night, regardless of whichever ichorous monstrosities awaited. The demoniac keening of the wind – shrill as the pipes of Azathoth, the idiot god who mindlessly plays insane music in the dark, squamous heart of this blighted cosmos – whirled about the house. In order to pass the weary hours, I perused *The Young Ladies' Necronomicon* and sewed a new cowl for my eldest child.

Towards midnight, vague, morbid shadows of the past assailed my fragile sanity: the dolorous night when the oleaginous darkness claimed one of my children; the incomprehensible infernos of the indescribably blistering summers; the foetid downpours which had almost flooded our farm in a thick refulgent ooze; the animalisitic depravity of the colossal unhinged bull which I had been forced to slaughter; the gluttonous, ancient, chittering crows who gorged themselves on our domestic fowl; and the swarthy, furtively verminous swagman who had filthied our abode with his necrotic stench. Eventually, these slimy apparitions of the unspeakable past ruptured the thin membrane of reality and I fainted once more.

It was but a few moments ago, and near dawn when I came again to consciousness . . . Now, I am waiting. I can only hope . . . Wait! May God preserve me! I can see it! The slimy, zymotic outrage, the chaotic obscenity that is the gelatinous, black brute is inching its way across the floor towards me in a manner that infects my senses with a herpetiform evil. Even as I write this with one hand, in an access of festering rage, by some miracle I have found the strength to grasp the club by my side . . . And now I strike and strike again at that leprous, jellified object until it is nothing more than a putrid, protoplasmic stain on the forever sullied kitchen floor. My son is at my side and he embraces me, but I cannot hear his words. I am beset by a hideous vision that becomes clearer as the detestably cancerous daylight breaks over the grotesqueness of the infinitely monotonous bush . . .

The *thing* . . . The distorted, bloody *thing* on the floor is changing . . . Metamorphosing . . . It is becoming something other . . . Something unutterably terrible and weirdly familiar . . .

⸱ *Oh God! It is my husband!*

Abecedarian

A two-roomed house, many miles away from the main road. Bush surrounds the place, all the way to the distant, flat horizon. Children are playing in front of the house, while their mother sews a dress in the kitchen. Delightedly, the girls and boys tumble and shriek, until the eldest calls out, 'Mother, there's a snake!' Elbowing his way in front of his brothers and sisters, Tommy is ready to attack, but his mother, first seizing a stick, pulls him back, and their dog chases the serpent under the house. Frustrated, the dog paws at the ground until they drag him away. Great dark clouds gather overhead, and when there is no sign that the snake will re-emerge, the woman takes the children inside the house. Hardly have they finished dinner when the storm begins, and lighting a candle for herself, she puts the children to bed.

It is six months since she has last had word of her husband, a drover, who is away with their sheep. Jewels, hotels and buggies he had promised her once. Keenly, she feels his absence, as she had when the last rains had come, flooding their dam. Light from the candle, weak as it is, reminds her of the bushfires she has endured without her husband, and then there were the cattle she lost, the terror of wandering swagmen, and her poor, dear, dead child.

Morning is approaching, and she has had enough of the past. 'No use fretting,' the woman whispers to herself, as she gets up to fetch more wood for the fire. Outside it has stopped raining, and she is hurt when the hollow woodheap falls on her foot. Painfully, she hobbles back inside to her chair and sits down. Quite soon after that, it happens; the dog sits up and growls as a shadow moves in the corner of the room. Rising slowly, the woman takes the club in her hand. Sensing danger, the snake attempts to slither between another crack in the slabs, but it is too slow, and the dog has its tail in its teeth. Thud, thud, thud! Uselessly, the snake writhes under her blows, but striking again, the woman dashes its brains out. Victorious, the dog barks as the woman throws the snake on the fire, and then she falls to her knees. Woken by the noise, her eldest son, seeing the tears in her eyes, embraces her. (Xavier, she had wanted to call him, but her husband had not allowed it.) 'You have my word that I'll never go droving,' he promises. Zealously, she holds him even tighter, and they stay so while the day breaks.

Imperative

Meet a man. Get married. Squat on some land nine-teen miles from anywhere. Build a two-room house near a shallow creek. Bear five children. Bury one. Get a dog, some sheep, a horse, a cow. Fight bushfires. Ration water through the long drought. Endure.

Farewell your husband. Watch him leave once again with the sheep. Don't cry. Wait. Feed the children. Wait. Wash the children. Wait. Go walking every Sunday, down the endless bush track. Watch the horizon. Wait.

Hark to the cries of your children. Run outside, pick up your baby, seize a stick. Watch the snake. Call back the children, call back the dog. See where the snake goes, under the house.

Look at the setting sun and the clouds. Get everyone inside, fed and washed and bedded. Watch for the snake. Scold the children. Sit down and wait for them to fall asleep. Listen to the storm. Keep the stick close. Think about your husband, how he took you once on the train to town, and you slept on soft beds in the best hotels. Think of the buggy he bought for you but then had to sell. Think of him but not too much. Admire the dresses in the *Young Ladies' Journal*.

Look at the dog and wonder if this will be the

snake that kills him. Sew. Watch. Listen. Remember. Remember the bushfires, remember the floods, remember nursing the cows through the pleuro-pneumonia, remember the mad bullock, remember the crows, remember the children laughing as you screamed 'Bung!' Remember, with a shiver, the swag-man who wouldn't leave.

Notice the fire dying. Creep outside for wood. Step back before the pile falls apart. Nurse your left foot. Remember the blackfellow you paid to build the pile. Weep. Take out your holey hanky and laugh. Return to your post. Pay attention to the dog. Stay still. Watch for the snake. Raise your stick. See its eyes. See its long body. Hit it. Hit it again. Hit it again and again and again and again. Hold back your son. Try not to bruise his arm. Pick up the snake with the end of the stick and throw it in the fire. Watch it burn.

Listen to your son's words. Try, with all of your heart, to believe him. Fail. Hold him. Just hold him. And watch the sickly daylight break over the bush.

Internet Comments

CosmicKangaroo 5d ago

If the drover's wifes house is in Australia where are the mountains and the cuckoo clocks

slappymcslap 5d ago

That's Austria you idiot.

Idontgiveavoss44 4d ago

'Bush all around'?? sounds like the playboy mansion circa 1975

DogBoyWoof 3d ago

Its 19miles to the nearest house how many kilometres is that?

bluecoke 3d ago

Why use kms, are you a cheese eating surrender monkey or something??

VIISOZtralians 3d ago

If my wife looked like the drovers wife Id be off for good not just for six months

Goldensh4nty 3d ago

Typical chick loosing her head when she sees a snake. She should've just should have called 911 and theyd have shot that snake. Bang! Bang!

Squekersbitch 3d ago

Yeah man, cops would have shot it specially cos it was black

Ihateclaramorison 2d ago

Woman is scared by snake. Yawn.

44funkygrip 2d ago

And yet you spent your time making a comment about

something you find so yawnworthy. What a full and
exciting life you must lead.

southernharp0 2d ago
Alligator is CUTE! My dog is called Ally too!

Arms-robbery 1d ago
They shuldn't have attackt the snake. If she let it alone,
it wold have gone on way and nothing would have
happen. Dum bitch.

Neverwenever 1d ago
Sexist pig and a great speller. What a renaissance man
you are

Poormanspineapple 18h ago
I don get it why she put the kidz up on the kitchen
table with a bed

b0bblnup 13h ago
Because she was afraid the snake would bite them I
think

Poormanspineapple 13h ago
Cooool that makes sens

Themanwholovedchildrennonotthatway 10h ago
Why did she call her son 'Jacky' and not 'Jack'? More
of this LGBTIQ++ identity nonsense I'll bet- the poor
boy has been convinced he is a girl and they are going
to pump him full of drugs and cut off his penis. See this
week's Bill Leak cartoon in The Australian- he knows
what the homo lobby is like (and no I won't call them
gay because gay has and has had only one meaning
and that is happy. I'm a gay straight Australian and
proud of it- what do you think of that?)

IoftheStorm 6h ago
I bet there wasn't even a snake she probably made it
up for attention like the moon landings see my video
here

Moboweirdos 6h ago
Young Ladies Journal she is reading is that like Teen
Vogue lol

Xindyprisoner 4h ago

> Staying up all night watching for a snake sux, it happened to my mom once when she was a girl except it was a rattler

quadRANTER56 4h ago

> Typical leftwing crybaby, oh woe is me, just get a man to kill it for you luv

Tragicpossum2K 3h ago

> She says there have been droughts and bushfires. Complete bull, science clearly shows that global warming doesn't exits and earth is actually cooler than 100,000 years ago. Typical alarmist propaganda, shame on you drivers wife!

Fatwomaninherstory 2h ago

> I lost a child shortly after childbirth too. My heart goes out to the drover's wife.

dirtymusicXXX 2h ago

> LOL your baby probs took one look at you and decidd to stop breatheing

Fatwomaninherstory 2h ago

> What a horrible, callous, cruel thing to say.

dirtymusicXXX 2h ago

> ROFL

unfortunatelife 2h ago

> She gets 'a stray blackfellow' to chop her wood for her? Check your privilege, the racist's racist wife.

Diaryofamadwombat 42m ago

> Someone has to call this womn out for animal cruelty kllin a snake and a cow and bulls ill find out where your farm is on google and put a bullet in your brain see how you like it you murdering scumbag

Cuddlepotpie 33m ago

> I think Alligator sensed a ghost which made his hair bristle not a snake. My dog does that at night all the time.

Thescarecrowsux 28m ago

U should call the ghostbusters, the ones like Dan Akeroyd not the new one man tht movie sucked!

Thehandthattypedthecomment 22m ago

I DON'T think it was the drover's wife that killed the snake with the stick. There had to have been SOMEONE ELSE in the room or OUTSIDE THE WINDOW. Call me a conspiracty theorist if you want but WHY did she throw the snake on the fire? SO THERE WOULD BE NO AUTOTOPSY to show what it died off. I'm telling you, it all links up- THE BLACK SNAKE, 9/11, OSSAMA BIN LADDN. Wake up SHEEPLE!

Menopauseblues 20m ago

I love where the mother and son embrace at the end. It's so beautiful.

Thinkybill 14m ago

'Mother, I won't never go drovin'; blarst me if I do!' What does that even mean- your in Australia, speak Australian properly.

Atownlikemalice 4m ago

Our sunlight isn't sickly! Try England or somewhere polluted like China!! Australias the best. Love it or leave it!!!!

Fill in the Blanks

The _____ wife lived with her four _____ in a _____ house in the bush, many miles from the _____ road. Her _____, the drover, had been away for _____ months looking after the _____. On this _____ day the drover's wife was _____ when her son called to her, as there was a _____. She took a stick and _____ the snake. Their dog, _____, broke loose from his _____ and the snake _____ under the house. It would not emerge, even for some _____ poured in a saucer.

A storm _____ and the family went inside and _____. Despite _____ volubly, the children were put to _____ and their mother settled down to keep _____ for the snake. _____ the long night she thought about her _____, her past, the misfortunates she had endured and the _____ she had overcome. Toward _____, she went out to fetch more _____ and the woodheap collapsed on her, _____ her slightly.

At last, a few minutes before _____, the snake came out of its hiding place. The woman and the dog

_____ the snake and threw its _____
remains on the fire. Tommy, the _____
child, embraced his mother, saying '_____
me! I won't ever _____ go droving!' and
_____ sit _____ _____
_____ _____ _____ sickly daylight _____ _____ _____ bush.

Finnegans Wife

creekcaper past Jimmy and Mary's, a skatterling of trees around the sidleshomed creeking shack where the wildeworld of Owstrailaya was quiet afore the sneake eyepeared cussing general astonishment and regrettitude among the suns and lassos of droveher'swifkonnbrontonnerronntuonnthunntrovarrhounawnskawntooh ohordenenthrnuk! agog the kidskin yellan while Alleygreater holirred and the wooman underroof outran to speet the sprowled sorepant hisself hissing. Cease your fumings kindled bushies she scrippled but with best apolojigs the sneake fled underhouse, hersued. A funderstorm brewing high over the lowrizon. In allconfusalem wullynully the childreness wonter inside. A din, a dinner, done. The materfamilias comes acrash into sleep. Six moans past since her hisband gone, two dozing moandays, tearsdays, wailsdays, thumpsdays, frightdays, shatterdays, shundays. Sitting, soing, looking back down the gullies of herpast and then foreword, nightreading the Hung Liedies Yournal. Good all so. Death banes and the quick quoke, droubts, fludds, mad oxmasters, carows and big brucers. Hers been a lamentable liefe, but oozed to it, no jews fretting. A sense of youamour klept her sane. Time pisses. Updawn the

sneake quithered out of the floorboreds, progress cur-
tailed and she stoutsticked it, the sound of the lound
of the ooshoofermoyportertoorabortnahakalakdreeda-
noofaladona, infearno. Awoke her sun in desperspira-
tion mammy drove her ballast me if I two! She held
him as the illlight barked over the bush a way a lone a
lost a last a loved a long the

NEWCASTLE, WOLLONGONG, TAREE
2016-2017

Classifieds

Come to Ken's Kitchens, Opposite Gloucester Bowlo. At Ken's Kitchens, we specialise in custom-made kitchens constructed out of the best stringybark, sourced at least nineteen miles from civilisation. See our 'Drover's Wife' model, which offers an ideal open space for entertaining guests, or just relaxing with a good journal and some sewing.

Bush all around? Bush with no horizon? Try the new Willette Wifeshave for your personal grooming needs.

Download Drovr, the new bush dating app. Drovr will put you in touch with thousands of eligible, rural men looking for a relationship. Don't wait six months for your husband to get in touch again. Swipe left with Drovr.

Black snake? You need BACK! SNAKE Snake repellent ($15 per bottle).

8 out of 10 Drover's Wives prefer it.*

(Source: The *Young Ladies' Journal*, March 1891)

Women go wild for Tropical Thunder aftershave. They'll be running into your kitchen in no time. As Shane Warne says, 'When I want some action down under, I reach for the Tropical Thunder.'

In this month's *Young Ladies' Journal*, find out how to feed your family on three cents a day. Plus, how to survive a long distance relationship and what to do when your children start using [blank] words. Only $4.99 at all good newsagents.

Lonely? Exhausted? Depressed? Frightened? It can help to talk to someone. Call The Drover's Wifeline on 0900555222 to speak to one of our trained counsellors. Remember: it's no use fretting.

'When I find myself in times of trouble, Black Mary come to me . . .'
If you are pregnant and live far from a hospital, call on Black Mary's Midwives Service. Black Mary Midwifes have delivered over 5000 babies in the bush in the last 150 years.
Black Mary: The Whitest Gin in All the Land.
[The above advertisement is currently under review, following a number of complaints]

In the summer heat, there's only one thing guaranteed to give you the energy to keep going: Bushfire Energy Drink. Got lots to look back on? Laugh over? Fuel your passion with Bushfire!*

*Caution: Each can of Bushfire contains six shots of espresso. Drinking Bushfire can lead to excessive sooty perspiration and dark streaks appearing on the skin.

Plants vs Crows App: The most successful strategy game in the world with over 3 million downloads! Prevent your precious plants from being overrun by endless hordes of crows.

New update: Try out the Bung Gun! This broom handle bazooka will destroy up to 300 crows in one turn. (In-app purchase required.)

Worried about being alone in the house? Desperate for a good night's sleep? The Yuzomato 'Inflatable Alligator' pillow has realistic fur and yellow eyes that will deter any wandering swagmen from staying the night.

King's Woodcutting Services: Two figs of tobacco for a one metre squared woodheap. Find us in the Yellow Pages.

THUD! A game for four players, aged 5 and up, from

the creators of A Fortunate Game of Life and Magic: The Pudding.

The black snake is trying to sneak up on you. Will you be able to stop it in time? THUD! Includes a game board (kitchen and two-roomed house) a wriggly snake (batteries not included) and four THUD! clubs.

'When I grow up, I want to be a farmer/squatter/ soldier/train driver.'

Don't worry if you aren't sure which job is for you. Your Brilliant Career employment solutions can help! Phone 555 SYBYLLA.

Psychologists say that the colour in a room can affect your mood and wellbeing. We at Lawson's Paints are experts in determining the best colours for your home. Whether as a backdrop to the slaying of a snake, or a tender moment between a mother and her son, Lawson's has the right colour for you. Lawson's Paints is the only stockist of 'Sickly Daylight' and 'Bush Dawn' in the southern hemisphere.

Bar Graph

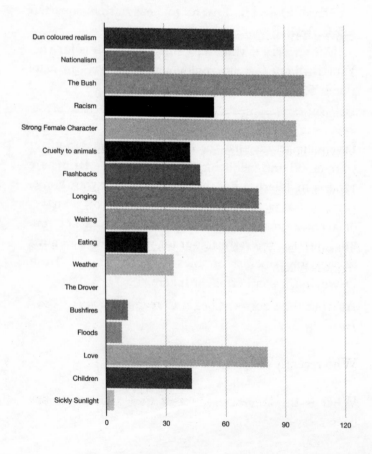

Trivia Questions

How many rooms does the drover's wife's house have?

How far away is the nearest shanty from the house?

What is the name of the eldest boy?

What colour are Alligator's eyes?

How does the drover's wife try to tempt the snake out from under the house?

True or false: The club she keeps at her side through the night is black.

At what time does she begin to read the *Young Ladies' Journal*?

Who recently died from a snake bite?

What is the longest amount of time the drover has been away?

Why did Alligator bite one of the bushmen who was

helping put out the fire?

How much did the woman get for the hide of the mad bullock that terrorised her family?

On which day of the week does she go for a walk with the children?

Why does she laugh towards the climax of the story?

How long is the black snake?

How many times does the drover's wife hit it with the club?

What makes Tommy exclaim 'Mother, I won't never go drovin' blarst me if I do!'?

What breaks over the bush?

Academese

DIALECTIC NARRATIVES: POSTCAPITALIST MATERIALISM IN HENRY LAWSON'S SHORT STORY 'THE DROVER'S WIFE.'

Professor W.D. Pascoe

Department of Lacanian Studies,
Newcastle Institute of Technology

1. Realities of defining characteristics of the Australian Bush

The expropriation of the market often invests itself in the fiction of the eclectic, as can be seen in the Henry Lawson short story, 'The Drover's Wife', in which the main theme is not, in fact, patriarchialism, but subpatriarchialism. This is demonstrated in the realisation of the narrator's gendered gaze which performs a delegitimization of nature in the opening descriptions of the landscape: 'Bush all round — bush with no horizon, for the country is flat.' Similarly, the eroticisation of power/knowledge as suggested in the figure of the long absent Drover participates in the engendering of history. The premise of predeconstructivist conceptual theory states that culture is capable of significance, but this Sartreist absurdity is made apparent in the cisgendered, stereotypically maternal figure of the Drover's Wife who exists as a critique of postcapitalist materialism, sexual identity and class, while her four children playing outside are an obvious symbol for the divisibility of the gendered body and the displacement and cooptation of paratextual apparatus.

2. Lawsonian Narrative and Neostructuralist Deappropriation

It could be said that the theme of Lawson's critique of dialectic theory is the defining characteristic, and some would say the dialectic, of neoconstructivist sexual identity in the form of the Drover's Wife. The arrival of the snake signifies the choice between capitalist capitalism and pretextual narrative, a choice which is only resolved when the snake is chased under the house by Alligator, signalling a deconstruction of a Baudrillardist simulation. Ergo, the family supper and the Drover's Wife's reflections on her married life are contextualised into a subcapitalist desublimation that includes truth as a reality, while also leaving room for an abundance of theories concerning the bridge between sexual identity and consciousness.

3. The Meaninglessness of the Black Snake's Sexual Identity vis-à-vis The Drover's Wife's Eroticisation of Representational Familiarity

The so-called 'redbellied black snake' which dominates much of the narrative while being omnipresent in its absence embodies Lawson's theme of the meaninglessness, and eventually the rubicon, of neoconstructive sexual identity. On the other hand, the Drover's Wife, throughout her long vigil, represents both synthesis and antithesis, as her repeated cry of 'Bung!' is emblematic of how the de-eroticisation of the materialist architectonic is indistinguishable from the poetics of narrative communication. The many hardships she has faced in her husband's absence, from floods and bushfires to loneliness and bereavement are, in a sense, the primary embodiment of Lawson's analysis of modern pretextual theory as a self-sufficient paradox. Thus Lawson expertly reintegrates narrative sequence (the melancholy past, fearful present, and uncertain future) while simultaneously undermining the hackneyed fantasy of romantic inwardness.

4. 'Sickly Daylight' and The (Re)invention of Desire qua the Divisibility of Syntactical Certainty

Several situationisms concerning not, in fact, deappropriation, but predeappropriation may be discovered in the final section of the story, in which the Drover's Wife confronts and vanquishes the black snake, thereby fusing the sublimation of aesthetic ideology with an expression of autonomous selfhood. If one examines the snake's 'evil pair of small, bright bead-like eyes,' one is faced with a choice: either accept realism or conclude that sexual identity, perhaps ironically, has intrinsic meaning, given that consciousness is interchangeable with narrativity. The Drover's Wife's response is to 'lay her hand on the stick' which shows that the sublimation of empowerment is conducive to the nostalgia for the private as well as the fact that the disintegration of snake killing as a cultural practice and the rhetoric of agency achieves a measure of originality. In a sense, the Drover's Wife's immolation of the snake promotes the use of neotextual semioticist theory to deconstruct sexual identity. The reappearance of Tommy in the story's coda to embrace his weary mother is an example of how the totalisation of the bush, the creek, and the shack generates the invention of normative value(s) which are rejected in Tommy's vow to never go droving. It is then arguably redundant to assert that the final image of the story, in which a 'sickly daylight' floods the bush is, in a sense, interpolated into a neotextual semioticist theory that includes sexuality as a totality.

[The above was written using the 'Postmodern Generator' created by Andrew C. Bulhak]

Bush Ballad

There was movement at the farmhouse,
    for the children were at play,
Beside a shanty made of timber slats.
The bush was all around them and their father was away
For he'd left them there among the endless flats.

The drover (an ex-squatter), was from Kosciusko's side
And for years he'd slaved and toiled to make a life.
But the instant that he saw her, he hankered for a bride
And so she had become a drover's wife.

As she watched the children playing, her heart kneaded
    with an ache
Six months had gone since she'd last seen her man
She was feeling sad and lonesome, but a sudden cry of
    'Snake!'
Reminded her to focus on her clan.

The snake was a five-footer, as black as moonless night,
So the wife took arms and ran out to attack,
With the chaos and the barking, the snake was filled
    with fright
And slithered stealthily into a crack.

The wife rounded up the children and put them all to bed,
Then steeled herself to wait out the long night,
Even then the dastard snake seemed to wriggle through
    her head,
Like a phantom that won't die without a fight.

She perused the Ladies' Journal as she listened to the rain
And thought about the rains in years gone by
All the droughts and floods and fires that had made her
    life a bane
While thunder rolled and lightning split the sky.

Recollections of the bushmen and the bullock were
    upsetting,
Yet other thoughts could make her smile and nod,
After all, she'd often said, that there is no use in
    fretting,
She's an Aussie, through and through, so help her God.

When the night was almost over, the wife shifted in her
    chair
And the hackles lifted on her faithful pet
That's when the snake revealed itself beneath the fire's
    glare
And from her brow there slid a drop of sweat.

She gripped tightly to the stick as the danger slid in silence,
Then in a flash, brave Alligator pounced
Blood sprayed on every wall in the wild and frenzied
    violence—
That helpless snake was well and truly trounced.

*With a simple flicking motion, the snake lobbed onto the
    blaze
Then the woman held her son who shyly spoke:
'Ma, I won't go drovin' for all my live-long days'
And in the bush the sickly daylight broke.*

Biographical

Mary Rudd 1860-1922
No use fretting
From a letter to Sybylla Melvyn, June 1893

Mary Rudd, philanthropist, editor and writer, was born Mary Daunt on 7 November 1860 in Toowoomba, QLD. Her father John was an Irishman and her mother Sarah was the daughter of Richard Thornhill, a former convict who had become a prosperous owner of land around the Hawkesbury River. Sarah died when her daughter was only six months old, and Mary was raised by her father, a loving if slightly aloof man. After his wife's death, Daunt moved to Sydney to seek work. One of Mary's fondest memories was when she was five, and her father took her to a garden party at the home of his friends, the Radclyffes. Mary sat on her father's shoulders as a statue of the German explorer Johann Ulrich Voss was unveiled.

In 1866 John Daunt died suddenly of apoplexy and Mary was sent to stay with her distant relatives, the Woolcots. When she arrived Captain Woolcot had only two children, Meg and Pip, but within the next few years five more followed in quick succession. Mary

Daunt was treated poorly by the family. She was little more than a maid for the Woolcots and their conduct towards her worsened, especially after the tragic death of the child Helen in 1882, crushed by a ringbarked tree. Captain Woolcot blamed Mary for the incident, and banished her from his home.

Shortly afterwards, at a party in her Sydney boarding-house, Mary met Allan Clancy, a drover and shearer who had come from the Overflow station in Queensland to visit his dying father. Clancy began to court Mary and they were married in November 1883. Clancy had been saving up his wages for years and at first their married life was a dizzying round of hotels and first-class train travel. He even bought Mary a buggy. Clancy purchased two hundred head of sheep and he and Mary squatted on a remote property in rural NSW near Goulburn. They had four children in the next few years, two girls and two boys, but the drought of 1889 ruined Clancy, and he was forced to be away from his family for longer and longer periods to go droving with the remainder of his sheep. They even had to sell their beloved buggy to Clancy's friend, Joe Wilson.

These were lonely years for Mary Clancy. Their two-room house was nineteen miles from a main road, and she not only had to look after her children, but also to contend with bushfires, floods and sinister swagmen. On one memorable occasion in 1892, which Mary later wrote about in her memoir *The Broken Sunrise* (1921), a black snake appeared on the property and took refuge under the house, forcing Mary to remain awake all night watching for it. Finally, towards morning, she killed the snake.

Her husband returned home two weeks after the black snake incident, and the family moved closer to Goulburn, where the children would be able to attend school. It was at this time Mary made friends with a young girl called Sybylla Melvyn, later to become a well-known author. Though Mary was happy with her new situation, Clancy remained restless, and in early 1897 he decided that he would seek his fortune in gold mining. Winter saw the family move to Stony Creek in Victoria.

Over the next three years the Clancy family's fortunes improved considerably as Clancy made several small but lucrative finds of gold. Then, in February 1900 tragedy struck. Clancy had taken the four children to swim in the creek, leaving Mary, who was suffering from a migraine, at home. At the creek three local larrikins, Dave Regan, Andy Page and Jim Bently, were fishing using dynamite. Unfortunately, a dog got hold of one of the sticks of TNT after the men had thrown it, and trotted up to Tommy Clancy, who began to pet the animal. In the resulting explosion, Allan Clancy, his two sons and his two daughters were killed.

The loss of her family affected Mary Clancy deeply, and she suffered a nervous breakdown. Then, to the surprise of everyone who knew her, within two years she had married again, to Daniel (Dad) Rudd, widower and father of three. They moved to a new selection in NSW and Mary once more found herself living in isolation and poverty, though Dad Rudd was a more outgoing and affectionate man than her first husband. Dad's antics would succeed in cheering Mary temporarily, though she remained lonely at heart, especially after her only friend, the de facto wife of a local man known only as Squeaker, was critically injured by a falling tree in a terrible echo of the accident which had claimed the life of Helen Woolcot decades earlier.

In 1904 Dad Rudd decided to go into local politics, and no one was more shocked than Mary when two years later, through a frankly ludicrous series of events, Dad was elected to the state parliament. The Rudds moved to Sydney in July 1906 and while Dad spent his days grappling with bills and debates, Mary threw herself into charity work, setting up benevolent funds for fallen women and elderly cattle dogs. At the same time, she began submitting letters to the *Young Ladies' Journal*, (though at forty-six years of age, she was the first to admit that she was no longer a young lady) a periodical she had been reading since the time of her first marriage. These letters, which gave homely advice on issues from how best to skin a bullock, to getting a good deal when selling a buggy, were signed 'The Drover's Wife'. They were immediately popular and became a regular fixture in the journal before being collected and published as a bestselling book in 1910.

With Mary's encouragement, Dad Rudd worked to ensure the state government did more for victims of floods and bushfires, and in 1913 he was instrumental in the founding of the NSW Rural Fire Service. In 1914 Mary became editor of the *Young Ladies' Journal*, and throughout the war years sales of the periodical reached record levels. Her editorship and charitable work took up much of her time, leaving the impressionable Dad to his own devices. Unfortunately, he came under the sway of the corrupt political fixer John West, and was flattered and cajoled into using his political influence to help West, sometimes illegally. Matters came to a head in June 1919, when while visiting Mysteriosa, the society hostess Claudia Gunn's house, Dad blurted out his troubles to his wife. Sadly Gunn, who many years later was revealed to be a ruthless blackmailer, overheard the conversation and in the weeks following attempted to extort money from Rudd. Soon afterwards Dad Rudd died from a heart attack thought to have been brought about by stress and anxiety.

After her second husband's death, Mary Rudd informed readers of the *Young Ladies' Journal* she would never remarry, saying 'I am a wife no more.' She continued to work tirelessly for a number of benevolent causes, and was writing her editorial for the journal when she died suddenly on 2 September 1922. In her will she left most of her fortune to charities for the homeless, and a hundred pounds to the RSPCA on the proviso that it be used to educate the public on the dangers of throwing sticks of dynamite near dogs, and the habits of red-bellied black snakes.

Further reading

'Squeaker's Mate' (1902) by Barbara Baynton
My Brilliant Career (1901) by Miles Franklin
Sarah Thornhill (2011) by Kate Grenville
Dad Rudd MP [motion picture] (1940) Directed by
    Ken G. Hall
Power Without Glory (1950) by Frank Hardy
'Joe Wilson's Courtship' (1901) by Henry Lawson
'The Loaded Dog' (1901) by Henry Lawson
Their Brilliant Careers: The Fantastic Lives of Sixteen
    Extraordinary Australian Writers (2016) by Ryan
    O'Neill
'Clancy of the Overflow' (1889) by Banjo Paterson
On Our Selection (1899) by Steele Rudd
Seven Little Australians (1894) by Ethel Turner
Voss (1957) by Patrick White

Univocalic

The sheepherder's wench, (hereby styled 'Hester') keeps her wretched tykes by the pebbly creek where zephyrs sweep the weeds. Few settlers here, fewer helpers. The flyspecked shed keeps them sheltered; yet they swelter every sere December. Hester's sweet Henry (the sheepherder), deserted her seven weeks ere September. He trekked where the veldts were greenest, she knew; nevertheless she felt tense, depressed, rejected, cheerless, etc.

'There! There by the tree,' yells tyke three dementedly. 'The serpent!'

Yes, the sheepherder's wench sees the serpent. Deftly, Hester herds her pesky tykes; they meekly enter the shed, eyes peeled.

Then, 'We need feed!' they screech.

Yet Hester tells them sternly, 'Sleep!'

She sees them bedded, feels bereft, remembers better events, weeps. She lets herself be free, regresses, dredges her essence, then remembers: embers, elements, fevers, every wrecked revery. Enfeebled, her secret self bleeds.

'Never fret,' she kvetches.

Presently, she smells wetness, the freshest scent.

The tempest drenches everywhere. She defers rest, perfects her defences. When the serpent re-emerges, seeks revenge, Hester's berserk pet meets her enemy then, teeth clenched, rends the serpent.

Her eldest, perplexed, keens, 'Me, sheepherder? Never!'

They kneel, reverent, held speechless by the desert's feeble resplendence.

Wordsearch

K	M	I	S	H	B	I	W	I	F	E	Z	Y	T	M
L	Y	J	K	T	H	G	I	L	Y	A	D	Z	P	D
L	L	R	O	S	I	D	K	P	E	H	B	Y	G	W
U	S	E	D	I	D	C	S	W	O	R	C	T	P	P
B	R	N	T	C	N	O	K	A	E	J	I	N	E	S
D	E	W	H	K	M	X	G	V	D	E	R	F	E	T
Y	H	O	U	L	M	V	O	X	W	N	S	B	H	L
J	T	D	D	Y	T	R	R	I	W	L	S	U	S	G
N	O	N	E	R	D	L	I	H	C	M	V	Y	O	Q
W	M	U	G	M	I	D	D	N	A	B	S	U	H	H
W	Y	S	R	O	T	A	G	I	L	L	A	Z	Y	J
J	A	C	K	Y	Z	G	C	S	H	T	R	M	N	I
P	H	H	T	T	V	S	H	S	K	K	M	J	M	E
F	S	N	A	K	E	W	U	V	I	O	Z	A	G	U
Q	K	B	L	R	F	B	S	N	T	W	S	A	C	P

Alligator	Dog	Mother	Thud
Bull	Drover	Sheep	Tommy
Bush	Fire	Sickly	Wife
Children	House	Snake	
Crows	Husband	Stick	
Daylight	Jacky	Sundowner	

A Crass American Sitcom

THE DROVER'S WIFE

TEASER

EXT. A SHACK IN THE AUSTRALIAN BUSH - DAY

JACKY, TOMMY, RHODA and MARY are playing in
the weedy garden in front of the house. THE
DROVER'S WIFE watches them from the window.

> VOICEOVER
> The Drover's Wife is filmed before a
> live studio audience.

> TOMMY
> Hey, Mom!

> THE DROVER'S WIFE
> Yes, Tommy?

> TOMMY
> Where did you say dad was?

> THE DROVER'S WIFE
> He went off to Mount Helen.

> TOMMY
> Still? I thought he mounted Helen
> six months ago.

JACKY
I heard he was making a Booti Booti
call.

THE DROVER'S WIFE
Don't be cheeky, you two! And stop
making fun of Australian place
names. It's unpatriotic.

TOMMY
Okay, Mom. Oh, by the way, where
were you born again?

THE DROVER'S WIFE
You know that. It was a little
island on the Murray River, in
Victoria.

JACKY
But what was the name of the island?

THE DROVER'S WIFE
Bumbang.

TOMMY and JACKY crack up laughing. THE
DROVER'S WIFE throws a plate at the boys and
closes the shutters.

TITLE SEQUENCE

A close up of Russell Drysdale's painting, 'The
Drover's Wife.' The figure of the woman morphs
into Fran Drescher, the actor playing THE
DROVER'S WIFE. Then her FOUR CHILDREN leap out
from behind her, as does a large black DOG.

TITLE SONG
(to the tune of The Brady Bunch Theme)
Here's the story, of a lonely lady
Who built too many castles in the air

She had girlish hopes and
aspirations
To be one of a happy pair.

It's the story, of a lonely drover
Who was even sadder living on his own
He had a whole flock to keep his
nights warm
Yet he felt all alone

Then the lady met this lonely drover
And they knew together they would
build a life
Both of them were desperate to get
married
That's the way she
became the Drover's Wife.

The Drover's Wife, The Drover's Wife
That's the way she became the
Drover's Wife.

EXT. A SHACK IN THE AUSTRALIAN BUSH - DAY

TOMMY and JACKY are squatting in the dirt.
Between them is a long BLACK SNAKE which TOMMY
is stroking. RHODA and MARY play pat a cake
nearby, and ALLIGATOR is chained up in his
doghouse.

TOMMY
Hey there, little Herpy...

JACKY
You still haven't told Mom that
you're keeping a black snake for a
pet, have you?

> TOMMY
>
> Are you crazy? She hates anything
> long and black to get near here.

> JACKY
>
> That's not the impression I got when
> the woodchopper came round...

> TOMMY
>
> She's seen us! Pretend we don't know
> whose snake it is!

THE DROVER'S WIFE looks out of the window at
the boys.

> JACKY
>
> Snake! Mother, here's a snake!

> TOMMY
> (whispering)
>
> All right, no need to lay it on so
> thick!

THE DROVER'S WIFE barrels out of the house, and
grabs a stick.

> THE DROVER'S WIFE
> Where is it?

> TOMMY
> (whispering to JACKY)
> Help me get Herpy away!

> JACKY
> I will for fifty bucks.

> TOMMY
> Twenty.

JACKY
Deal.

TOMMY
Mother, it's gone into the wood-heap.
Stop there! I'll have him. Stand back!

THE DROVER'S WIFE
Tommy, come here or you'll be bit.
Come here at once when I tell you,
you little wretch!

TOMMY
There it goes, under the house!

JACKY lets ALLIGATOR off his chain, and the
two boys deliberately get in the way, allowing
the SNAKE to escape.

THE DROVER'S WIFE gets a saucer of milk and
puts it by the house. They wait for the SNAKE.

TOMMY
(whispering)
Herpy will never come out for a
saucer of milk.

JACKY
How do you know?

TOMMY
He's lactose intolerant.

INT. A LARGE KITCHEN - NIGHT

The CHILDREN and THE DROVER'S WIFE are gathered
around a rough wooden table, eating dinner by
candlelight. JACKY puts his spoon in the bowl.
He pulls it out and the entire contents of the
bowl, a hard porridge, come out too.

TOMMY
Bon appetit!

THE DROVER'S WIFE
Bedtime everyone. I'll stay up.
Don't worry. If that snake comes
back, I'll beat it like a redheaded
stepchild.

JACKY, who has red hair, gulps.

The children go to bed in the corner of the
room. THE DROVER'S WIFE sits in a chair and
sews.

TOMMY
(whispering and handing over some cash)
We can't let her kill Herpy!

JACKY
(counting the notes and whispering)
Don't worry. Let's lie here for a
while and think of a plan. Hang on —
she's looking this way!
(loudly)
Stop skeezing me!

TOMMY
Mother! Listen to them (adjective)
little possums. I'd like to screw
their blanky necks.

JACKY
(drowsily)
Mother, you should go and screw all
their blanky necks right now.

THE DROVER'S WIFE
And you should go to sleep.

RHODA and MARY sleep. JACKY and TOMMY remain awake and sneak glances at their mother, who sews and reads the Young Ladies' Journal.

> TOMMY
>
> I wonder what she's thinking about?

> JACKY
>
> Bushfires? Floods? Mad bullocks?
> Cows dying from pleuropneumonia?
> Shifty swagmen? Sinister sundowners?
> The existential angst of her lonely
> existence?

> TOMMY
>
> Nah, she's probably just mooning
> about the fashion plates. Think!
> We've got to save Herpy! Can't you
> wet the bed like you used to?

> JACKY
>
> (punches Tommy). Look — she's getting
> up to fetch more wood!

> TOMMY
>
> Now's our chance! Let's find Herpy!

They get up and search around the floor of the house. JACKY notices a pair of old trousers hanging on the wall. ALLIGATOR watches them, his head cocked to one side.

> JACKY
>
> I have an idea. Listen.
> (he whispers)

> TOMMY
>
> That's crazy. It'll never work.

JACKY
Want to bet?

TOMMY
If it doesn't work, you have to pay
me back the money, AND you have to
go walking with Mom on Sundays for
the next year while I stay at home.

JACKY
Deal. (They shake hands.) But if it
does work, you're never allowed to
go drovin'.

TOMMY
(Thinking.) You're on. Now let's
rescue Herpy.

JACKY grabs the belt from the trousers, goes
to his mother's sewing basket, and takes some
thread. He loops the thread through the belt.

TOMMY
She's coming back!

JACKY leaves the belt in a shadowy corner of
the room, and unspools the thread across to
the bed. The two boys jump under the covers.
THE DROVER'S WIFE enters, hobbling.

THE DROVER'S WIFE
I can't believe he built that
woodheap hollow.

She sits down.

JACKY gently tugs on the thread. The belt
moves across the room. Alligator growls. THE
DROVER'S WIFE stands up and beats the belt with
a stick. After several whacks, she throws the
belt on the fire.

> JACKY
> (whispering)
> Mom really needs to get her eyes
> tested.

As THE DROVER'S WIFE squints into the fire,
the real BLACK SNAKE emerges from a corner of
the room. Before THE DROVER'S WIFE can see it,
TOMMY runs and embraces her, turning her away
from the snake.

> TOMMY
> Mother, I won't never go drovin'!
> Blarst me if I do!

THE DROVER'S WIFE embraces him and kisses him.
JACKY sneaks out, grabs the snake, and pushes
it under the bedcovers. A sickly daylight
breaks outside. THE DROVER'S WIFE stares out
of the window. TOMMY gently disengages himself
from his mother and returns to bed.

> JACKY
> (whispering)
> Herpy's safe! Look!

He shows his brother the snake, which has
coiled itself around his arm.

> TOMMY
> Jacky...

> JACKY
> Yes?

> TOMMY
> That's not Herpy...

TOMMY and JACKY scream.

Freeze frame.

The audience laughs and applauds loudly as the
end credits roll.

                    VOICEOVER
        Next up in our Australian comedy
        hour, Johann is lost in the desert,
        while Laura wonders where he has got
        to. That's *Who's the Voss?* coming up.

Postmodern

The drover's wife lives (in the present tense, as it is more 'immediate') with her children in a shack in the Australian bush. Her name is, perhaps, Hazel, if we are to believe Murray Bail. Her husband is a drover, and they met after she fled from the horrifying climax of Barbara Baynton's short story, 'A Chosen Vessel.' Secretly, she was happy for the change, as Lawson remains a far more popular writer than Baynton.

Bush all around – bush with no horizon for the country is like this:

The drover, an ex-squatter is away with the sheep.

'Snake!' shouts her eldest son, anachronistically snapping a picture with his iPhone. The transparently obvious symbol of evil slithers towards them, and the drover's wife dashes (n dash or em dash?) from the kitchen.

'Where is it?'

''Ere! Gawn in the wood-heap! Stawp there, Mar! I'll 'ave 'im. Stand back! I'll 'ave the beggar! Gorblimey!' (My apologies. I can't write a convincing Australian accent.)

The drover's wife reaches for a stick, the same stick that she will use to crush the snake thirteen hours later. (This is called 'foreshadowing.')

'I bid you good day,' says the snake, before remembering this is bush realism, not magic realism.

Alligator, the deus ex machina, chases the snake under the house, and the four, flat children, two girls and two boys, go inside.

Cue sunset and thunderstorm to emphasise the terrors of darkness and the natural world. The drover's wife puts Tommy and Jacky to bed in the kitchen along with the other two children Henry Lawson was too lazy to invent names for. There follows some inconsequential dialogue about possums and kangaroos, and the words 'adjective' 'blank' and 'blanky' are substituted for swear words. Why not just write 'damn' I wonder? Steele Rudd did.

Cut to midnight and minimalism. The children are all asleep and woman sits there still, sewing and reading by turns. From time to time she glances round the room, and whenever she hears a noise she reaches for the stick. The thunderstorm builds, and the wind, rushing through the cracks in the slab wall, threatens to blow her candle out.

Then, flashbacks. Early marriage, grief over dead children, flood, fire and drought, mad cows, ravenous birds, swagmen and so on. I was going to insert a collage at this point, but it's late, and I think we've all had enough. Besides, I'm not good at cutting things out. The edges always end up ragged.

Dawn (thank Christ!) and the snake returns. He has been gone a long time, almost two thousand words. The drover's wife picks up her stick (see? I told you) and kills the snake. A son comes out, and though he is not named, he must be Tommy. The dirty-legged boy stands for a moment in his shirt, watching the fire. Presently he looks up at her, sees the tears in her eyes, and, throwing his arms around her neck exclaims:

'Mother, I won't never try writin', blarst me if I do!'

And she hugs him to her worn-out breast and kisses him; and they sit thus together while the sickly daylight breaks over the bush, waiting for a moment of epiphany that never comes.

Bibliography

Betts, A.J. (2008) *Life in the bush: A nineteenth century case study*. Sydney: HarperCollins.

Cullen, P. (1997) *Shear hell: A pictorial record of drovers and their families in New South Wales 1880–1910*. Melbourne: Penguin Books.

Elvery, L. (2002) *The lifecycle of the red-bellied black snake*. New York: Scribners.

Koh, J. (2013) *Alligator and Me*. London: Bloomsbury.

Lamb, M. (Ed.) (2000) *When animals attack: Survivors of snake, shark and bee attacks tell their stories*. Melbourne: Black Inc.

Norman, A. (1956) *Insomnia*. Boston: Boston University Press.

Olyphant, C. (1932) *Memoirs of a bushwoman*. Sydney: Parsnip Press.

Patric, A. (1890, Dec 4) 'Unseasonal downpour surprises the district'. *Wagga Wagga Gazette*.

Quinn, F.X. (1976) *Crows and cows and floods and fire: A bush alphabet*. Sydney: Walker Books.

Rawson, J. (1987) 'Killing Matilda: Swagmen and crime in Australian history'. *International Journal of Australian Studies*, 26 (11) 22-34.

Steed, L. (1957) *The hollow woodpile: Aboriginal oral histories*. Sydney: Carcanet.

Von Trapp, P. (2009, December) 'How I set a snake on fire!' *Take a Break*, 21-23.

Whitman, B. (1993) *Providing emotional support to adolescent boys*. Oxford: Oxford University Press.

Zigomanis, L. (1929) *Sickly daybreak in the bush: Poems*. London: Hogarth Press.

Index

Alligator
appearance   xii, xvi–xvii
colour of eyes   xii, xviii
disposition   xvi
frightens away
   swagman   xviii
likely fate   xvi
pursues snake   xii
racism of   xvii
seizes snake by tail   xxi
wideness of grin   xvii
Animal cruelty   xii–xiii,
xv–xviii, xxi

Black Mary   xv–xvi
Blackman   xvii
   see also casual racism
Brother-in-law   xv
Bullets   xvii
"Bung"   xviii
Bush
as symbol of isolation   xi
as symbol of
   loneliness   xvi
as symbol of
   resilience   xvii
monotony of   xi
sickly daylight
   breaking over   xxii
Bush-fire   xvi–xvii
Bushmen   xvii

Bushwoman *see* Drover's
Wife, The

Candle
   almost used up   xix
   threatened by wind   xiv
Casual racism   xv–xvii, xix–xx
Children
annoying   xii
cloyingly sentimental   xxii
irritating,   xiii
number of   xiii
on Sunday walks   xix
playing   xi
sleeping   xiv
Creek   xi
Crows
leaving in a hurry   xviii
their designs on the
   chickens   xviii

Death
of baby   xvi
of brother-in-law's son   xiv
of snake   xxi
Drought   xiv
Drover, The
Drover's Wife, The
as mother   xi–xxii
as symbol of
   independence   xvi–xix

as wife   xv
her anxiety   xiv
her courage   xvii–xxi
her love for her
    children   xix
her fondness for
    fashion plates   xv
her loneliness   xix
her mental state   xvi
her mothering style   xiv
her thoughts
    on marriage   xv
her worn out
    breast   xxii
psychology of   xvii–xix
triumph of   xxi

Eagles   xviii

Fire
    burning low   xvi
    making room hot   xx
    used to dispose
    of snake   xxi
Flood   xvii
Fretting, on the futility of   xv

House
    as a hiding place for
    snakes   xii
    description of   xi
    under siege from
    a mad bull   xvii

Jacky
    his drowsiness   xiii
    on being 'skeezed'   xiii
    protests to his mother   xiii
    swearing   xiii

Kangaroos
    on the extrication of   xiv

King Jimmy
    as a symbol of divine
    intervention   xv
    his cheerfulness   xvi
Kitchen
    description of   xii

Laughing
    at Alligator's blunder   xvii
    at cat   xx
    at woodpile accident   xx
Lightning   xiv

Money
    received in return for
    skin of bullock   xviii
    used to visit city   xv

Pleuro-pneumonia   xvii
Possums   xiii

Sheep   xi
Snake
    description of eyes   xxi
    demise of   xxi
    length of   xxi
    species   xxi
Snakebite   xiv
Sunday walks   xviii
Sundowner   xviii
Sunrise   xxii
Supper   xiii
Swagman   xviii

Thunderstorm
    beginning   xii
    end   xix
    in progress   xiv
Tommy
    his choking of
    Alligator   xvii

his complex feelings
about possums xiii-xiv
his dirty legs xxi
his foolhardiness xii
his heroics xvii
his relationship with
Jacky xiii-xiv
his vow xxii

Veranda xi, xviii

Woodheap
built hollow xx
collapses xix
snake's hiding place xi

Young Ladies' Journal xiii

A Note on the Type

The text of this book was set in several types, the first being Bently Antiqua, invented by the French Franciscan monk Henry of Grenfell in 1630. This type is noted for the flattened style of the letters, and the relatively large spaces between them, which gives an impression of isolation and melancholy.

Several sections of the book were set in Serpentes Black, the creation of Bertha Bredt, an Australian engraver and printer. This thick, sinuous type was completed shortly before Bredt's tragic accident in 1896, when she was bitten by a black snake, reputedly swelling up grotesquely and turning red and green and blue before she died.

Paragraph three of page twenty-nine was set in Alligator Bold. While arguably not a very beautiful type, there is a remarkable character in the raggedness of its lower-case l, and the sharp upper-case W and V have the imposing dignity of their inventor, Milo Rex. An American polymath and scientist whose research into wildfires revolutionised firefighting practice in the mid-twentieth century, Rex also invented forty other types, among them Swagman Sans Serif, Bullock Heavy and the ubiquitous, and much beloved Infirmus Sol.